A Swan House
Ballet School Mystery

Milly, Spencer, Lottie and Merv return to Swan House for another term of ballet and Spy Craft – and thanks to the talented Helen Lipscombe, we're all invited too! Hurrah! The trouble is, the Mouse King is also here for the reunion – and (according to my investigations) he's an infamous villain who has his sights on a dangerous treasure. Plus, the new Head of Ballet and his annoyingly perfect daughter are acting . . . well, rather suspiciously. Can Milly separate what she's *really* seeing from what she *wants* to see? This spy stuff is more complicated than it looks. I'm off to practise my *jeté* in preparation – *au revoir*!

BARRY CUNNINGHAM
Publisher
Chicken House

TROUBLE in a TUTU

A Swan House Ballet School Mystery

Helen Lipscombe

Chicken House

2 Palmer Street, Frome, Somerset BA11 1DS
www.chickenhousebooks.com

Text © Helen Lipscombe 2020

First published in Great Britain in 2020
Chicken House
2 Palmer Street
Frome, Somerset BA11 1DS
United Kingdom
www.chickenhousebooks.com

Cover and interior design by Helen Crawford-White
Typeset by Dorchester Typesetting Group Ltd
Printed and bound in Great Britain by CPI Group (UK) Ltd, Croydon CR0 4YY

The paper used in this Chicken House book is made
from wood grown in sustainable forests.

1 3 5 7 9 10 8 6 4 2

British Library Cataloguing in Publication data available.

PB ISBN 978-1-912626-96-0
eISBN 978-1-913322-52-6

For Mum and Dad

CAST

At Home

Milly Kydd	*Student ballerina and spy*
Eva Kydd, 'O'	*Milly's mother – prima ballerina and secret head of Swan House School of Ballet*
Catherine Lilova, 'Bab'	*Milly's Russian babushka*
Max Deverall	*Ballet dancer and choreographer*
Leonora Deverall	*Max's daughter*
The Bombardier	*Milly's next-door neighbour*
Boris	*Milly's cat*

At Swan House School of Ballet

THE STUDENTS

Lottie Li	*Milly's best friend*
Benedict Spencer	*Milly's friend*
Merv Crump	*Head of IT and Milly's friend*
Willow Perkins	*Milly's nemesis*
Amy Bee, 'Bumble'	*Willow's best friend*
Tom Garrick	*Injured year eight*
Fleur Fontaine, Dipti Patel, Danny Debello	*Other year eights*
Jada Gayle	*Head Girl*
Dafydd Wynn-Jones	*Head Boy*
William Flynn	*A sixth-former*

THE VIRTUAL MENTORS

The young Filipp Popov	*Milly's mentor*
The young Nora Doone	*Lottie's mentor*
The young Ivan Korolev	*Spencer's mentor*

THE STAFF

Ms Celia Sitwell	*Director of Swan House School of Ballet*
The Captain	*Spy Craft teacher*
Madame de La Cloche	*Disgraced ex-Head of Ballet*
Madge Little	*Shoe Keeper and doobrie inventor*
Hugo Kinsmeet	*Retired Shoe Keeper*
Emmeline Topping, 'Topsy'	*Housemistress*
Cook	*Topsy's mother*
Sid	*Virtual librarian*
Nurse	*Sleeping draught specialist*

At Meekes the Shoemaker's

Mr Stubbs, 'Heart Maker'	*Milly and Eva's shoemaker*
Mrs Huntley-Palmer	*Shop manager*

Other spies

Ivan Korolev	*Ex-Swan House student, founder of the Korolev Dance Academy*
Kristina the Knife	*Korolev's star pupil*
Trevor Topping	*Cook's husband and Topsy's father – Swan House agent. Deceased.*

1

'Twas the Night Before Christmas

Shots ring out. Swords slice the air. One by one, dancers fall.

My skin tingles. It's like I'm right there. Onstage.

The Nutcracker *jetés* and my feet flex. Clara *relevés* and my toes point. When they defeat the evil Mouse King, Mum and Bab cheer. I squeeze Mum's arm and her muscles tense. She's thin, but Mum's a ballerina. And ballerinas are stronger than they look.

'Milly, come closer.' Her whisper kisses my cheek. 'This reminds me of an important rule in *The Guide to Espionage* about never giving up – try, try, try again. I wouldn't be here today if I hadn't followed that rule.'

Darkness wraps her shoulders like a shawl and the battle onstage glints in her eyes. I remind myself Mum's not just a ballerina.

The lights go up for the interval. 'Vhat a vonderful evening. Isn't the Prince to *diiie* for?' Bab winds a feather boa around her neck. 'Christmas simply isn't Christmas vithout *The Nutcracker* and it's even more perfect now that ve're together again – that calls for champagne!'

'And ice cream?' I say, blinking myself back to earth.

'And ice cream, dahhling. You can have anything you vant – it's Christmas Eve!'

My babushka takes my hand, still tingly from clapping, and we wind from our box to the stairs.

People make way for Mum. She swishes past the black suits and silky dresses in a long white gown studded with jet-black beads. I'm wearing the new dress and silver high-tops Bab bought me last term, 'for the Christmas party at your new school'.

Turned out Swan House School of Ballet wasn't that kind of school. Spy schools don't do parties.

I find the ice-cream queue in the foyer, and listen to murmurs of 'Isn't that Eva Kydd?' follow Mum to the bar.

I smile to myself. After 364 days of being kidnapped, she's home. And not just for Christmas Day. For the whole of the Christmas holidays. That's two whole weeks of just Mum, Bab and m—

There's a tap on my shoulder.

'Millicent?'

I know that voice. My legs want to scarper, but not as much as the rest of me wants to see the Dance of the Sugar Plum Fairy in Act Two.

I stick my smile back on and turn around. 'Oh, hi, Willow. Are you enjoying the show?'

Willow Perkins rolls her violet eyes. 'Did you see the duel between the Nutcracker and the Mouse King? Sooo lame. And Davina – that's my dad's fiancée – says Clara was *très gauche*. Honestly. Even you could do better.'

That's Willow trying to be nice. I try to be nice back. 'Ice cream?'

Her nose wrinkles. 'No, thank y— OMG! Don't look now, but Max Deverall's behind you.'

'*The* Max Deverall?' I peek over my shoulder, hoping to see the superstar dancer turned superstar choreographer. 'Where is he?'

'Too late, you missed him.' Willow's face is a picture of smugness, like one of those tiny dogs that gets to ride in their owner's handbags. 'Anyway, I'm glad they found your mother. The papers said she had amnesia.'

I practise my unreadable spy-face. 'Yes. She was looked after by a very nice family in Piccadilly or thereabouts. Bab says it happens all the time.'

I score myself a two out of ten on the fib-o-meter,

5

but Willow's not even listening – she's got her own news.

'Did I tell you Davina has her very own drama school in LA?'

'What flavour would you like?' says the ice-cream boy.

'Strawberry, please. Um, LA?'

Willow swishes her blonde ponytail. 'You know – Hollywood. She says it won't be long before my acting is as good as my dancing. She says I'm going to be a star.'

I'm not surprised. Acting and lying are almost the same thing, aren't they?

Willow lowers her voice. 'And given that I almost died last term, I've decided spying's not for me. So I don't suppose I'll see you again.'

I peel off the lid of my ice cream. 'I don't suppose you will.'

'You'll see me, of course, on the silver screen.'

I scoop out a pink creamy dollop and suck on the small, wooden spoon. How many miles are there between Hollywood and London? Must be thousands. Next to having Mum home, that's the best Christmas present ever.

Willow waves at a woman in a long black dress. 'Here's Davina. Divine, isn't she? Guess this is *adieu* then, Millicent.'

'Guess it is. *Bon voyage*, Willow.'

The woman kisses her cheek and I realize I'm happy for Willow Perkins. I really and truly am.

I take my seat in the box, snuggle into the dark and wait for the Sugar Plum Fairy.

Mum puts down her programme. 'I hope Bab comes before it starts. I'd forgotten how long it takes her to powder her nose.'

We clap for the conductor. The orchestra waits for his baton to twitch but there's a noise. Not the tinkle of a harp or the toot of a flute – a *whoosh*. A *whizz*. A *KER-RACK*.

Like bonfire night.

One of the cellists squeals. A squiggle of neon shoots through the air, hangs over the orchestra and bursts in a shower of stars. The lady playing the celeste swats a spark from her hair. There's a scream from the stalls below and my stomach squiggles too.

Mum jumps up.

'What is it, Mum? Is it part of the show?'

'I doubt it, sweetheart, and I don't think we should stay to find out. Hold my hand. We've got to find Bab.'

Mum's hand is cool and dry. Mine is hot and

sweaty. It's only been three days since I stopped Filipp Popov from blowing up Swan House. To be perfectly honest, I've had enough excitement for one week.

Another rocket explodes over our heads. Fiery sparks rain down. My heart gullumps.

People are clambering over their seats, charging down the aisles.

'Milly, this way!' coughs Mum.

Smoke creeps up my nose. We run out of the box and into a stampede of dark suits, silky dresses, pointy elbows.

Gull-ump. Gull-ump. Gull-ump.

Wrapped around her wrist like an almost invisible bangle is Mum's Swanphone. She holds it to her lips and whispers a command. The next thing I know her voice is booming over the screams and clacking heels. It's Mum on loudspeaker.

'PLEASE REMAIN CALM. MOVE SWIFTLY TO THE EXITS AND TAKE CARE ON THE STAIRS.'

We move against the crowd. I lose Mum's hand. A heel stabs my foot. We keep pressing forwards. Then down. And down. And down.

Mum bursts into the Ladies. '*Mama, ty gde?*'

I shout too, 'Bab, where are you?'

No reply, just a tinny recording of 'The Dance of

the Sugar Plum Fairy'. One by one, we crash into the cubicles.

'She might have gone outside,' says Mum. 'Let's go!'

I take one last peek in the loos and run after her.

2

The Deveralls to the Rescue

We reach the crowd fighting to escape through the revolving doors.

I search for Bab's feather boa as Mum speaks into her Swanphone. Her voice echoes around the lobby. 'WOULD CATHERINE LILOVA PLEASE MAKE HER WAY QUICKLY TO THE EXIT.'

Bab never makes her way quickly anywhere. She's not going to start now – not in her high heels.

Mum lets go of my hand. 'Milly, wait for me outside. I'm going back in.'

There's a *whizz* and a *bang* over my head. Clouds of grey smoke curl around the spotlights.

'I'm coming with you!'

'Please, sweetheart, stay here. Your babushka will be fine, I promise. I'm sure this is just a silly prank.'

Mum turns but the crowd barrels us through the doors and we spin on to the icy pavement. There's a laugh behind us.

'You always did have perfect timing, Eva. Here, I've got something for you.'

'Max!' says Mum, brushing herself down.

Max?

I twirl around. Bab is in the arms of a man with autumn hair and bonfire eyes. I wipe the sleet from mine. Willow was telling the truth for once – it's Max Deverall. He puts Bab down like she's wearing glass slippers and kisses her hand.

Bab purrs. 'My knight in black tie. Aren't we lucky that Max happened to be in the audience tonight, Eva?'

'We are indeed,' says Mum, pulling Max aside. 'You can explain what you're really doing here later. Are you thinking what I'm thinking – this isn't a Code Pink?'

A Code Pink? Is Max Deverall a superstar spy too? I listen extra hard.

Max whispers, 'Yes, but if I'm right about who's behind this evening's entertainment, we can't take any chances.'

'Then let's go.' Mum drops his arm. 'You finish clearing the area. I'll check for hidden devices.'

'You're the boss. Just one moment.' Max calls over our heads, 'Leonora!'

A girl appears out of nowhere. She has the same autumn-streaked hair, but hers falls all the way to her waist. 'Yes, Dad?'

11

'Keep an eye on the exits. If you see anyone acting suspiciously, follow them but don't get too close until you hear from me, OK?'

The girl nods.

'Milly,' says Mum. 'Stay with Bab. Don't move from this spot.'

Mum and Max dash back through the doors.

'Wasn't that Eva Kydd with Max Deverall?' says an old lady standing next to Bab.

Bab smiles. 'Yes, Eva's my daughter. Don't they make a vonderful couple?'

A vonderful *vhat*? I slip on a frozen puddle.

Bab and the old lady start talking about Mum and Max Deverall like they're Made For Each Other. My feet start to walk.

Sirens wail as I follow Leonora Deverall on to Bow Street. I wish she'd slow down – after my fight with Filipp Popov, my ankle still throbs when I run.

'Your mom asked you to stay with your grandma,' says Leonora in the sort of accent that's lived in and out of a suitcase.

'I just want to help,' I say in the sort that's never left Clapham.

Leonora's eyes dart from face to face. 'Look, Milly, you did awesome work at the Scarlet Slippers, and don't take this the wrong way, but right now you're just a distraction. Please go back.'

Who does Leonora Deverall think she is? She might be taller than me, but she doesn't look any older. She stops dead and I have to go up on my *demi pointes* to see what she's staring at.

A man in a scarf and hat.

Doesn't look very suspicious to me.

'What is it? Why are you looking at him?'

Leonora doesn't answer. He crosses the road and she follows.

I traipse after her. 'Leonora!'

No answer.

'LEONORA. Why HIM?'

The 'him' looks straight at me.

Oops. Didn't mean to shout.

He backs into the side of a car, raps on the window and jumps inside. The engine revs. Leonora chases after it and I chase after her. A bike zooms between us, splashing brown slush all over my new dress.

'Rats,' says Leonora as the car turns a corner.

My face burns. I should have stayed with Bab. I wait for Leonora to shout at me but if she's cross, you'd never know. She has the best spy-face I've ever seen.

I mumble an apology.

'It's OK,' she says. 'I'd have followed you if it had been the other way around. At least I got the number plate.'

I kick the kerb – why didn't I think of that?

'And look,' she says.

Leonora runs to the middle of the road and returns with a small, black umbrella.

Nothing very suspicious about that either. 'Why did you follow him?' I ask.

'Didn't you see his gloves?'

'His what?'

Leonora sighs. 'Come on, your grandma will be wondering where you are.'

A flurry of snow chases us through the police cordon. A policewoman holds up her hand. 'Wait a minute, you two.'

Max Deverall jogs towards us and flashes his super-star smile. 'It's all right, Officer. They're with me.'

Behind him, blue lights flash in Mum's eyes. 'Milly, what happened? I asked you to stay here.'

I glance at Bab but she's still chatting to the old lady. 'Sorry, Leonora thought she saw a man—'

'He got away, but he dropped this,' says Leonora.

Mum takes the umbrella. 'Thanks, we'll check it for fingerprints.'

'Description?' asks Max.

I shrug. 'His face was hidden by a scarf.'

'A black scarf,' corrects Leonora. 'He was about five eight, a hundred and forty pounds. Wearing a black coat and hat. His hair was covered by the hat, but his gloves were singed. There were holes in the fingers. I'm pretty sure his fingertips were singed too. I figured he'd been handling gunpowder.'

Blimey. Leonora must be half owl.

A smile flickers on Max's lips. 'That's my girl.'

'He got in a car,' says Leonora. 'I've forwarded the number plate to Control.'

I glance at her wrist. She's wearing a Swanphone just like Mum's.

Mum buttons up her coat. 'Good work, Leonora. Now that the police have taken over we should get back.'

A taxi stops for the old lady and Bab takes Max's arm. 'Vhat have I missed? Vhere are you staying, Max? Vill *Mrs* Deverall be joining you later?'

'It's just the two of us,' says Leonora. 'Mum died when I was a baby.'

Bab reaches for Leonora's hand. 'Forgive me, dahhling, I had no idea.'

Instictively, I reach out too, but Leonora backs away. 'It's OK, it happened a long time ago. Dad and I have booked a hotel . . .'

Bab gasps. 'A hotel? On Christmas Eve? Dahh-ling, I von't hear of it!'

15

'Neither will I,' says Mum. 'You must stay with us.'

WHAT?

Max glances at Leonora. When she smiles I see someone else in her face. I can't think who.

'Are you sure?' he asks Mum.

'Absolutely. There are just the three of us at home. It would be our pleasure, wouldn't it, Milly?'

I nod the tiniest nod and look down at my new shoes, all ruined.

They're not the only thing.

3

The Unexpected Guests

Mum throws her house keys on the kitchen table.

'Sorry everything's rather bare. We didn't have time to put decorations up this year.'

I look around the kitchen. No tinsel. No tree. No presents. This morning it didn't matter. We were still going to have the best Christmas ever.

I kick off my wet shoes. This morning feels like forever ago.

'I don't mind, it's really cosy,' says Leonora, warming her hands over the range. 'I love all your stuff . . . the dresser . . . the fireplace, and that old grandfather clock in the hall. It's cool, isn't it, Dad?'

'Sure is,' says Max, but you can tell he's not listening. His eyes flick from the ceiling to the larder. From the door to the garden. They fix on the window. He pulls back the blind and peers into the night. 'Thanks

again for having us, Eva. We've been living in and
out of hotels for a couple of years.'

'Five, actually, Dad,' says Leonora.

'That long, huh? We still have the best time
though, don't we, Leo? We've just been in Shanghai.
Boy, that was –' he winks at Mum – '*fun.*'

Bab kicks off her heels. 'Vould you like a drink,
Max? Girls, be angels and bring two extra chairs
from the dining room.'

When we come back, Leonora asks if she can sit
next to me. I mutter a yes – sort of under my breath,
so she has to ask again.

Max is holding a glass. One with a gold rim Mum
keeps for best. Inside is something gold and icy. He
swirls it around and it tinkles like sleigh bells, smells
like old bog.

'Thank you, Catherine. *Cycni venustas, cor
leonis*!'

My eyebrows shoot up. *Grace of a swan, heart of
a lion.* He shouldn't be quoting the Swan House
motto in front of Bab. I look at Mum but she's
searching through the larder.

Bab raises her glass. '*Za lyubov!*'

To love?

Huh.

Leonora raises her fizzy water. I cross my arms.
Max loosens his bow tie and sits next to his daughter.

His fingers rap the table top, his knees jiggle under it. Mum's keys begin to jingle and my nerves begin to jangle.

'Dad's not very good at sitting still,' says Leonora.

'He was the same in school. In fact, he hasn't changed at all . . .' Mum checks the date on a packet of nuts. 'Sorry, we don't seem to have anything to eat.'

I frown. 'I didn't know you were at school together.'

'Only in the last year,' says Mum.

Max gets up and starts to explore the kitchen, picking up our things and putting them down again. He stops at the mantlepiece and reaches for my Scarlet Slipper trophy.

'You were quite the *étoile* last term, Milly.'

Bab sighs. 'She vas the star of the show. I only vish I'd seen her vin.'

'Sorry, Bab,' I say. 'I should have asked someone to film it.'

Actually, I had other things on my mind at the time. I was trying to stop my dance partner from blowing Swan House sky high.

'Don't vorry, dahhling,' says Bab. 'Perhaps that adorable friend of yours – Spencer, vasn't it? – perhaps he remembered.'

She pats my hand as Boris squeezes through the

cat flap and stares at Max. His neck bristles like a fat, ginger loo brush.

Mum laughs. 'Sorry, Boris isn't the friendliest cat.'

'It's OK. I'm more of a dog person,' says Max. 'Cats have no loyalty.'

I bristle on Boris's behalf and pat my knees. 'Boris, come here.'

Boris squishes between my legs and jumps on Leonora's lap. She tickles his ears and he purrs.

Traitor.

Bab pours a nip of vodka into a tiny glass and sets it on the mantlepiece. 'For Ded Moroz,' she explains to the Deveralls.

'Isn't he the Russian Father Christmas?' says Leonora. 'We were in Moscow a few years ago – I thought the Russians celebrated Christmas in January.'

'They do,' says Mum. 'But we're in England now.'

'Ah, but ve still do some things the Russian vay, don't ve, Mila?' Bab winks at me and nods at the dresser.

I jump up. 'Ooo, yes, it's Christmas Eve and you haven't told our fortunes yet.'

Mum and Max swap secret looks. Mum lays her hand on Bab's. 'It's too late now. Let's do it another night.'

'But dahhling,' says Bab, wrapping a tea towel

around her head like a scarlet turban. 'Ve have guests and it's so much fun!'

Max raises an eyebrow. 'That suits you, Catherine.'

'Not *Catherine*, dahhling,' says Bab with a twirl. 'Tonight I am Madame Yekaterina, fortune teller to the rich and infamous.'

Mum sighs. 'I'm sure Max and Leonora don't believe in fortune telling, Mama.'

'Come now.' Bab drapes her feather boa around Mum's shoulders. 'Vhere is your sense of fun?'

'Please, Mum,' I say. 'We didn't do it last year because you weren't here.'

'And I'd love to have my fortune told,' says Leonora.

Bab's eyelashes flutter. 'There. You are outnumbered, Eva. Mila, pass me a candlestick and a platter from the dresser. And four sheets of paper too.'

'Yes, Madame Yekaterina!'

I put everything on the table. Mum gives in and switches off the lights. Max taps his foot as the grandfather clock in the hall strikes eleven.

A match is struck and the flame wavers under Bab's chin. Her Cleopatra eyes grow larger than ever. Excitement flares in my stomach.

'Mila, you vill go first. Show our guests vhat to do.'

I scrunch a piece of paper on the large earthenware

21

dish and watch Bab set it alight. It curls and crackles in the darkness. Mum raises the candle and Bab squints at a shadow forming on the wall.

'What are you doing, Madame Yekaterina?' asks Leonora.

'If you are very qviet, the shadow vill show me Mila's future,' whispers Bab. 'There – can you see? A ballerina. And she's dancing so beautifully.' Bab waves her hand at the mantlepiece. 'It is obvious, Mila. You are destined to vin another Scarlet Slipper.'

I study the dancing shadow. I think I see a ballerina wavering *en pointe*, but she doesn't look like a winner to me.

'Now you, Leonora,' says Bab.

Leonora's paper flares and the shadow leaps. 'Ahh, look!' Bab exclaims.

Leonara cranes her neck. 'What can you see?'

'Another dancer, and she is vhirling very fast. You vill also vin a Scarlet Slipper, dahhling.'

'That's so cool. You next, Dad.'

Max's eyes dance in the candlelight. 'I'd rather not know what the future holds. I like surprises – you know that, Leo.'

'Go on, it's just for fun. Please, Dad.'

Leonora gives Max some paper. Reluctantly, he watches it smoulder until the flames graze his fingers. It lands in the bowl with a crackle.

22

'Ahh,' says Bab. 'I see a heart. How vonderful – you vill find love, dahhling.' She gives Mum a twinkling smile. 'And now it's your turn, Eva.'

Mum tosses her scrunched-up paper in the plate. I cross my fingers behind my back.

No hearts, Bab, please. Mum doesn't need to 'find love', especially not with Max Deverall.

Bab claps. 'I see a svan – no vait.' Her hands fall to her sides. 'It's a plane – or a car – I can't tell.' She swirls around and her smile wobbles. 'Whichever it is, it seems you vill be leaving us again, dahhling.'

'No she's not!' My voice wobbles too. 'It's just a silly game.'

Ashes drift into the air as Bab unravels her tea towel turban. 'You are right, Mila. I think it is time for bed, don't you? After so such much drahhma, I need my beauty sleep.'

She gives each of us a kiss on both cheeks. It leaves lipstick on Leonora's. Perfume on mine.

As her footsteps reach the landing, Max closes the door silently, like he wants to keep Bab out. Keep his secrets in.

'At last, we can talk.' He joins Mum at the table and refills his glass. 'Welcome to the fold, Milly. You've probably guessed Leonora and I are spies.'

'Yes, but how come you know Mum is the head of Swan House? I thought that was top secret.'

Mum answers for him. 'Max and Leonora have clearance at the highest level. They're two of our most valuable agents.'

'You're not so bad yourself, Eva.' Max gives her a square-jawed grin. 'It's not easy being a prima ballerina by day and "O" by night. And now it looks like we've got even more competition – Milly, I heard you found your mother, saved the school *and* caught the bad guy.'

He tousles my hair and I smooth it down. 'I didn't catch him. He escaped.'

'I only know half the story,' says Leonora. 'What happened?'

'Let me explain,' says Mum, reaching for my hand. 'After Filipp Popov kidnapped me, he managed to pass himself off as one of the shoemakers at Meekes. He hid a bomb inside the Scarlet Slipper trophy and smuggled it into Swan House. On the night of the final, he disguised himself as Milly's dance partner but she saw through him. She fought him and they fell in the lake. They were both pulled out but Filipp tried to escape. Unfortunately the water was too cold . . .'

'He didn't survive?' says Leonora.

I shake my head miserably.

'Don't waste your tears on Popov,' says Max. 'He knew the risks. It's what being a spy is all about – the danger, the excitement, the cut and thrust of it all.' He slices the air with an invisible sword. 'That's why we love what we do, right, Leo?'

My eyes begin to sting. Mum and I have gone over this. I don't want to talk about Filipp Popov with Max and Leonora Deverall. Not on Christmas Eve. Not ever.

Mum gives my hand a squeeze. 'Milly was very brave, but what's done is done. Let's get back to tonight. I assume your presence at the Opera House was no coincidence, Max.'

'You're right, Eva. Girls, I don't need to tell you that what I'm about to say goes no further.'

Boris's ears prick up. Leonora nods and sets down her glass.

'Milly?' says Max.

I roll my eyes like Willow Perkins. 'I can keep a secret.'

Max turns up his sleeve. 'A couple of days ago, I received an anonymous message on my Swanphone.' He points his wrist at the table. 'Look at this.'

Boris stops purring and fixes his sharp, green eyes on the tiny figure shimmering next to Max's glass.

It's a hologram. A tiny virtual mouse, wearing a tiny virtual crown.

The mouse bows to Max and starts to speak in a tiny, squeaky voice.

'Twas the night before Christmas,
And all through the house,
The children were stirring,
And so was a mouse.
A gift he had plotted,
And planted with care,
In hope that the black and white swan would be
there.
He sat down and waited among the fine folk,
And laughed as the Sugar Plum went up in
smoke.'

The mouse laughs a tiny, squeaky laugh, then vanishes in a puff of virtual smoke.

Mum's cheeks are white. 'It can't be.'

Max lowers his wrist. 'Sorry, Eva. The Mouse King – he's back.'

4

The Mouse King

'The Mouse King?' says Leonora.

'Like in *The Nutcracker*?' I ask.

'Yes, sweetheart.' Mum rubs her temples. 'He hasn't been active for years. I thought he was dead.'

'So did I,' says Max. 'But this has his MO all over it. Remember how he loved to play games? As soon as I heard all that stuff about the night before Christmas and the Sugar Plum, I knew he was planning something at the Royal Opera House.'

I spot the worry on Mum's face before she smoothes it away. 'And the black and white swan – I suppose he means me?'

'He must do, those roles in *Swan Lake* made you famous. Planting the fireworks is his way of telling Swan House he's back.'

Leonora stiffens next to me. 'This Mouse King, is he dangerous?'

Mum nods.

'And do you think the man outside the theatre might have been him?'

Max drains his glass. 'Possibly.'

'I shouldn't have let him get away!'

Leonora's cheeks are snow-white but mine are on fire. 'It was my fault. He only ran because *I* shouted.'

Max's eyes flicker and Mum's turn away. No one can look at me, not even Boris.

Some Christmas Eve this is turning out to be.

'Happy Christmas, sweetheart, you're up early.'

The kitchen clock says ten to seven.

Mum holds out her arms and gives me a hug. Her hair is pinned in a shiny knot at the nape of her neck. Her dress is the colour of Christmas. It nips in her waist and puffs out her hips. Jingling around her wrist is the silver charm bracelet that helped me to find her. She looks lovely.

'I found enough ingredients to made some *kozulya* – they're still your favourites, aren't they?'

Little Russian biscuits that look like reindeer are cooling on a rack next to the range. The kitchen smells like Christmas even if it doesn't look like it.

'Where are Max and Leonora?' I ask. Maybe they left in the night – that's what spies do, don't they? I cross my fingers behind my back.

'Still sleeping, I think. They flew from Shanghai yesterday. I expect they're still jet-lagged.'

I pull away. 'When are they leaving?'

'I don't know, Milly. You don't mind them being here, do you?' Mum tucks my hair behind my ears. 'You know, I think it suits you short.'

I twirl the longest strand around my little finger. 'When you disappeared and I thought I'd never dance again, I cut it off with the kitchen scissors. I hated it when I started at Swan House but it's grown on me now.' I pull myself on to the worktop. 'Mum, can I ask you something – why didn't you tell me you were a spy?'

Mum sighs. 'I couldn't, Milly. I haven't even told your babushka.'

'But we could have been a team, like Max and Leonora.'

'Sweetheart, the last thing I wanted was to put you in danger. To be honest, I'm still not happy about you returning to Swan House. Now that you've won a Scarlet Slipper there are lots of ordinary dance schools who'd love to have you. Think about it.'

I think about it for two and a half seconds.

'I want to go back. It's true I didn't like Swan House at first, but that changed when I made friends. They'll look out for me.'

'Friends?'

'Lottie, Merv and Spencer.' I blow on a *kozulya* and pop it in my mouth. 'You'd love Lottie, she's so funny and she's a black belt in kung fu.' Plus she's always getting into scraps, but Mum doesn't need to know that.

'And Merv's super clever and a genius inventor . . .' Of gadgets he keeps secret from the teachers. No need to mention that either.

'And Spencer's really brave and knows every single rule in *The Guide to Espionage*.' He says you have to know the rules before you can break them. Better not tell Mum that either.

Mum brushes a crumb from my cheek. 'All right, I won't stop you going back as long as you—'

The front door clicks open. There's a shout and my shoulders slump.

Max squidges through the door with a Christmas tree on his shoulder. A trail of pine needles follows him into the kitchen. 'Merry Christmas, ladies!'

He props the tree next to the window and suddenly the kitchen smells like Lapland.

'Where on earth did you find a tree on Christmas Day?' asks Mum.

Max taps his nose. 'Contact in the US Embassy. Leo and I couldn't turn up for Christmas empty-handed, could we?'

Mum laughs. 'It's enormous!'

'It's a pot plant compared to the pines in Finland. We spent a whole winter training there once – boy, that was a cold Christmas, wasn't it, Leo?'

Leonora staggers in with a large cardboard box. 'Freezing! But so beautiful. It was like living in Narnia.'

Shanghai, Moscow, Finland . . . Where haven't they been?

Smiling at Mum, Leonora plonks the box on the table and takes out chocolates, chutneys, chestnuts, cheese . . . a Christmas cake covered in icing. My stomach rumbles.

'Goodness,' says Mum. 'It's like Fortnum's has come to Clapham.'

Max backs out. 'There's more outside. What's Christmas without the trimmings, huh?'

Bab's voice sings from the hall, 'Don't you adorrre a man vith trimmings?'

My mouth says no. My stomach says yes.

Max comes back with another box and a huge sprig of . . . Boris yelps as I stumble over his tail.

Mistletoe. What do we need that for?

'I'll hang it in the hall,' says Max.

'Dahhling, vhat fun!' Bab nods at Mum and winks three times. Luckily, Mum's too busy filling the fridge to notice her behave like a loon.

'Are you all right, Mrs Lilova?' says Leonora.

'Perrrfectly,' says Bab. 'This is turning into a very merry Christmas indeed!'

'More Bolly, dahhling? How vonderful!'

Max fills Bab's glass until it's brimming with bubbles. 'What's your poison, Bombardier?'

'A tot of port,' says our next-door neighbour. 'Purely medicinal, of course – find it helps the digestion. Excellent bird, Eva. Beats a tin of minestrone, what?'

'You're welcome,' says Mum, clearing his plate. 'We couldn't have you eating alone on Christmas Day.'

Bab nudges the Bombardier's elbow. 'Mila, the Bombardier has something for you.'

'Ahh, yes.' The Bombardier pats his tweedy pockets. 'That new school of yours is on a lake, isn't it? Thought this'd come in handy.'

He digs out a brown-paper parcel. I pull out the contents and practise my unreadable spy-face.

'It's perfect. Thank you, Bombardier . . . er, what is it?'

'A sou'wester. What every young fishergal needs.'

'How charmingly . . . yellow,' says Bab in her chirpy voice.

32

Across the kitchen table, Max's face lights up. 'So you're a fisherman? Tell me, where's the best place to fly fish –' his eyes flick at Mum rinsing plates under the tap – '*north* of the border?'

Honestly, why did Max have to go and bring up fly fishing? Once the Bombardier starts talking about trout, he won't stop. Anyway, don't you have to be old to be interested in fishing? Or have a large twirly moustache?

'Can I go now?' I ask Bab.

'Just a second, Milly,' says Leonora as Mum sits back down. 'We got you presents too.'

She gives Bab a leopard-print scarf. Mum a rose-scented candle. Me a fine, silver necklace.

I roll my eyes. Exactly the kind I would have chosen for myself.

'Shall I put it on for you, Milly?' asks Mum.

'No thanks, I'll try it on later.'

Her forehead wrinkles at me then unwrinkles at Leonora. 'I'm sorry we don't have anything to give you in return.'

Leonora smiles. 'Oh, being here is ten times better than presents.'

I roll my eyes again. I seem to be turning into Willow Perkins.

Mum leans over and hugs Leonora like she used to hug Willow. I remind myself that she's just being kind

33

but I can't help going all hot inside. The hug lasts so long, I have to accidentally knock my juice all over Leonora to prise them apart.

'Oops.' I try on my sou'wester as she runs upstairs to change.

Bab yawns loudly. 'Fishing is so dull, Villy. Come, let's play cards in the drawing room.'

Max's knees jiggle as he watches the Bombardier leave. 'Is he ex-army? Do you want me to check him out, Eva?'

Mum laughs. 'He's just a harmless old man.'

'In that case, I'm going to stretch my legs outside.'

Max steps into the garden and I shuffle my chair closer to Mum's. AT LAST I've got her to myself.

'Mum, we can still go to Winter Wonderland tomorrow, can't we? Just the two of us, like we used to. There's a new ride called the Ho-Ho-Helter-skelter.'

She's staring at the spot on the table where the Mouse King stood last night.

'*Mum?*'

'Of course . . . Sorry, sweetheart, I was miles away.' She glances at the silver necklace. 'Wasn't it kind of Leonora to give us presents? I've got something for you too.'

'Really? I thought you didn't have time to buy presents this year.'

Mum pulls something from the pocket of her skirt. 'I cheated. This is something I've had for a long time.'

Wrapped in pink tissue is a silver charm. It looks like a tiny hand mirror.

'It's to go on your bracelet.'

'*My* bracelet?'

'I'd like you to keep it, sweetheart. You've earned it.'

The charms tinkle as Mum takes off her bracelet and carefully slides it on to my wrist. I throw my arms around her neck and breathe in the warm scent of cinnamon and cloves.

'Thank you! It's the best present ever!'

The back door opens and Max stamps his feet, leaving clumps of ice on the mat. Cold air and the faint peal of bells follow him inside. He peers over my shoulder and my neck prickles.

'Is that a doobrie, Eva?'

A doobrie? I inspect the charm more closely.

'I was just about to tell Milly. It's a spy gadget called a boomerbang,' says Mum. 'Hugo gave it to me years ago.'

'Who's Hugo?' I ask.

'He was the Shoe Keeper at Swan House when we were at school. Madge Little took over when he retired.'

'He was always telling me off for something.' Max

stoops over like he's a hundred years old and waggles an imaginary stick. 'Deverall – put that doobrie down before you blow us all up!'

Mum's laugh is as tinkly as Christmas bells. 'You deserved it.'

'You're probably right,' says Max. He straightens into his usual perfect posture. 'I guess he's with the big Shoe Keeper in the sky now.'

'Not at all,' says Mum. 'He's alive and well.'

'Is he? Pity.'

Mum wipes her eyes. 'Stop it, Max, I liked him.'

'You liked everyone.'

I gaze into the tiny mirror. 'What does it do, Mum?'

'It boomerangs missiles back to where they came from. Ingenious, isn't it? Hugo made it especially for my bracelet.'

'Do you remember his retirement party?' says Max. 'Everyone was there – a gathering of the great, the good and the ugly. I've never seen so many old spies in Swan House.'

Mum shakes her head. 'It was such a shame about poor Trevor.'

'Topping was an idiot. He was bound to end up dead sooner or later.'

Trevor Topping? I know that name.

I think back to what Cook said last term. '. . . *my*

Trevor, that's Emmeline's pop – he was a spy until they got him . . . They found him in the hippo enclosure in London Zoo. They're only pygmies, but he was a small man . . .'

'You mean Topping as in Topsy, my housemistress?'

'Yes, sweetheart. Trevor was Emmie's father. It was very sad – she was only nine when he died. That's why I asked her Mum to start cooking for Swan House.'

'But what happened?'

'We're not really sure. The security cameras showed Trevor arrive at Hugo's retirement party but never saw him leave. They found his body in London Zoo the next morning. It's haunted me for years – he said he'd been working on something top secret and asked me to meet him after the party, but he never came.'

'Reckon he'd had too much punch,' says Max. 'Anyway, enough about Topping. Didn't you say Milly'd come across another old doobrie of yours on her adventures?'

My *adventures*? He makes Mum's kidnapping sound like a day at Winter Wonderland.

I glance at Mum and she nods. 'You know, Milly, the golden powder compact that turns into a drone. I'm surprised it still works. The DC20 was the first model of voice-activated comcorders – it only recorded for twenty minutes or so.'

'The drone was yours? And it films stuff? I didn't know that.'

Max draws up a chair. 'Eva was Hugo's favourite – she always had the best gadgets. Come to think of it, I haven't seen a DC20 since we did that job in Paris . . .'

Here he goes again – he and Leonora are such place-droppers.

'Do you remember, Eva, when Korolev almost fell from the top of the Eiffel Tower?'

Mum's eyes sparkle. 'He was lucky someone was there to rescue him.'

Max's eyes sparkle too.

Huh. Of course Max the Superhero was there to save him.

'You realize, Eva, if no one's filmed with the drone since we were in school, there's a chance it might have some old footage of us in Paris. Have you still got it, Milly?'

I look from Max to Mum. Two pairs of sparkly eyes focused on me.

'Sorry, I've lost it. Must have dropped it on my "adventures". You know, when Mum and I almost died.'

'Are you sure?' asks Mum.

'Of course I'm sure.' I score myself a seven out of ten on the fib-o-meter and stand up. 'I'm going upstairs to try on my new necklace now.'

Max shrugs. 'Did I tell you I've started collecting vintage doobries, Eva?'

I close the door behind me, and wrinkle my nose at the mistletoe in the hall.

How close were Mum and Max at school? If he's right about the drone – there just might be a way to find out.

5

The Lost Drone

Quiet as a virtual mouse, I close my bedroom door. The music box Lottie and Spencer gave me for my birthday is under my bed. I don't want Leonora to hear the tinkle when it opens, so I squeeze inside my wardrobe. The little key is already around my neck.

Nestled in the box, smooth and gold against the velvet lining, is Mum's drone. I flip the mirror open and light spills on to the floor where I threw my clothes last night. There's the hem of my new dress, all stained. The toes of my silver shoes, all scuffed.

'Show footage,' I say, half whisper, half command.

Nothing.

I give it a little shake. 'Show film?'

Still nothing.

'*Play* film,' I say.

There's a knock on my bedroom door. 'Milly, are you there?'

Leonora!

I hold my breath and drop the drone, blinking away the sudden darkness.

Minutes go by, then footsteps pad downstairs. She's gone, but at my feet, someone is whispering. I grope the folds of my dress and feel the drone. A face is staring out of the mirror. But it's not Max or Mum. It's Tom Garrick. The boy who gave me the drone last term.

'Rewind,' I say.

The film whizzes back to the start and begins to play.

'Testing . . . testing . . .' Tom squints into the compact, his snub nose almost touching the mirror. 'I *knew* it,' he hoots. 'This is the best doobrie ever! It doesn't just film stuff, it acts like some kind of key.'

Some kind of *key*?

'Look,' says Tom, sweeping back his greasy brown fringe. 'I've snuck into the sixth form common room. Gayle would blow her top if she could see me now.'

He releases the drone and it floats up, shining a bright light on a large room scattered with tables and chairs. I don't understand why he's so excited. The most interesting thing about it is the biscuit tin next to the kettle.

'Boring, right?' says Tom. 'But watch this . . . OPEN THE VIRTUAL LIBRARY!'

In the quiet of the wardrobe I hear my heart thump as the room begins to shimmer. I let out a gasp as bookcases appear along the walls, each crammed with hundreds of beautifully bound books – every one a hologram.

The drone zooms in on the categories – *Agents*, *Assassins*, *Ballets*, *Choreographers*, *Codes*, *Composers* . . . It's the most extraordinary library I've ever seen.

'Welcome to the Swan House Virtual Library,' says a voice.

The drone spins around and lights up a tall wooden ladder. Balancing on the top rung is a virtual girl in little round glasses. She has a pink Mohican, tartan leg warmers and a tutu held together with safety pins.

'Who are you?' says Tom.

'My name's Sid and I'm yer virtual librarian,' says the girl in an accent that matches her leg warmers. 'I havnae seen ye before. What's yer name?'

'My name doesn't matter,' says Tom. 'I'm here for a book.' I can hear the smirk in his voice.

The girl frowns. 'Yer not in the sixth form, but as ye seem to have clearance at the highest level, I have to gie ye anythin' ye want.'

'Just give me the most highly classified, dangerous book you've got.'

Sid narrows her eyes. 'That would be *The Secrets of Swan House, Ancient and Modern* by Lord Astus. Ye'll be the first pupil to borrow it.'

'Whatever. Just hurry up before someone comes.'

In the furthest corner of the library, one of the bookcases swivels around. On the other side are even more books – secret, classified, dangerous books.

Sid's ladder slides along the bookcases. She finds the copy Tom asked for, whizzes back and hands it over. 'Put it on the table,' she says. 'Then tell it to open.'

Tom sets down the book in a puff of virtual dust. The drone zooms in on a pale-blue cover. The title is written in tiny, silver letters – *The Secrets of Swan House, Ancient and Modern* by Frederick Astus. It's the kind of book I wouldn't open in a hundred dusty years.

'Are you sure that's it?' says Tom doubtfully.

'Aye. Now do ye want to look inside the wee book, or not?' snaps Sid.

She's beginning to grow on me.

'OK, keep your Mohican on. Book open!'

The cover flips open and in a flap of paper and blurry words, the pages turn all by themselves.

'Slow down,' says Tom. 'I can't read anything.'

The book seems to understand. It pauses, then slowly turns over each page. There are maps, drawings and chapter after chapter written in a jumble of letters and numbers I don't understand.

'This is no good, it's all in code,' mutters Tom as the book falls open on a diagram. It looks oddly familiar.

'Pause,' I say to the drone. 'Zoom in.'

I squint at the drawing. It's a circular floor pattern showing dancers the direction of steps across the stage. We use them all the time in ballet. But what's so 'dangerous' about a floor pattern? I look closer. The title is written in some sort of code too.

NSKA BLCN BSRE.

'Play on,' I say, but the only thing in the mirror is my face. I snap it shut. Mum said the drone wouldn't record for long. I suppose Tom must have filmed the library just before he hurt his ankle and left Swan House.

I put the drone back in my music box, lock it and tuck the key in my jumper.

I might have to share my house. I might have to share Christmas. I might even have to share Mum.

But I don't have to share everything.

I wake up with Traitor Boris scratching at my bedroom door.

'Happy Boxing Day, Boris. You can spend as much time as you like with Leonora today – I'm off to Hyde Park. A whole day with NO DEVERALLS!'

Boris mews as I pull on my thermals and thickest jumper. 'I know, but I'm not as furry as you – it'll be cold on the Ho-Ho-Helterskelter.'

I grab my ruined high-tops and run downstairs.

'Is that you, Milly?' calls Mum.

I find her in the living room, cradling a mug of tea. She folds her legs under her like a swan and pats the sofa. 'Come here. I need to talk to you about something.'

She's still in her dressing gown.

'Why aren't you ready? The queue will be huge if we're late.'

Mum shakes her head. 'I'm afraid Hyde Park will have to wait. I've got to go away.'

Scrunch. My insides fold like paper. Bab's prediction was right.

'Go *where*? You said you'd be here for Christmas. For ALL of Christmas.'

'I'm so very sorry, sweetheart, but Max has a hunch about the Mouse King I need to investigate.'

'The Mouse King?' My throat goes all sticky. 'But he's dangerous. If it's Max's hunch why can't he go?'

'It's my job. Besides, Max is needed elsewhere.'

'When will you be back?'

'I'm not sure. I'll stay in touch, I promise.'

'But what if something happens, like last time . . .'

'Oh, Milly, I won't be in danger. It's just a reconnaissance. Please sit down.'

She holds out her arms, but I stumble back.

'You wouldn't be going if it wasn't for the Deveralls, would you? You'd be here for the holidays with me and Bab.'

Mum's lips press together. 'It's not Max and Leonora's fault, sweetheart. Please try and be sensible.'

There's a cough in the doorway. 'What am I supposed to have done now?' says Max. I fold my arms. His smile says he's not even a little bit sorry.

'Nothing,' says Mum. 'Is everything all right?'

'Can we talk for a second, Eva? It's business – won't be long, Milly.'

I slam the door behind me and stomp down the hall. Where's Mum going? What's so urgent about Max's hunch? Why does she have to leave right now?

I pause mid-stomp. There's only one way to find out. I tiptoe back to the sitting room. The door is smooth and cool against my ear.

Max is talking. 'Don't worry about Milly, Eva. These kids are tougher than you'd think – look at Leo. You'll be back in a couple of weeks tops – I'll look out for her, I promise.'

A couple of weeks – that's ages! Then I hear something that sounds like a sob. Has Max made Mum cry?

I head to the kitchen – fast but casual, like the Captain showed us in Spy Craft. Out in the garden, I press close to the wall. My jumper snags on the ivy but I tug it free, then edge along the scatchy bricks until I can peep through the French door into the sitting room.

My breath fogs up the glass so I rub a little hole with my sleeve.

Max is wrapping his arms around Mum's back. She rests her head on his shoulder and he touches her shiny, dark hair. Ivy claws at mine.

Don't they make a vonderful couple.

I jam in a sob and swallow it down. The window mists up and Mum disappears, but I've seen enough. I stumble back through the kitchen, run down the hall, burst through the door and shout without caring who hears, 'Why can't *you* go looking for the Mouse King? Why does it have to be Mum?'

Max laughs. 'Trying to get rid of me already?'

'She's only just got back,' I yell, 'and now you're taking her away again!'

Mum wipes her eyes. 'There are things you don't understand, Milly. Max is being a great help actually – we've got some good news.'

Good news? I begin to sink, like I'm back in the icy lake. They're in love. They're getting married. Max and Leonora are moving in. They're not just staying for Christmas – they're staying for half-term, Easter, summer, *for ever*?

Garghhh.

Mum puts her arm around my waist. 'Max has agreed to be the new Head of Ballet at Swan House until we can find a replacement for Madame. Isn't that great?'

I come up for air and take a big gulp. So they're not getting married. Max is going to teach at Swan House – that's not so bad . . . is it?

'So even though I won't be around for a little while, he'll be looking out for you.' She gives me her brightest smile.

'What about Leonora?'

'She'll start school with you in January,' says Max. 'Poor kid. School's going to be a bit of a drag after years of working in the field.'

Mum says, 'You know how it feels to be the new girl. You'll take care of her, won't you, sweetheart?'

'Of course she will,' says Max, ruffling my hair. 'But you don't need to worry about Leo. She's more than capable of taking care of herself.'

I try to smooth it down, but it's tangled. Everything's all tangled.

6

Return to Swan House

Apart from the shivering trees, Regent's Park is deserted. I stare out of the back window while Max whistles some soppy tune from *Romeo and Juliet*. Even though it's freezing, he's rolled down the roof. I pull my beret over my ears.

We drive past the lake in a car Ms Celia sent over this morning. Her favourite rule from *The Guide to Espionage* is 'Never judge a car by its bonnet'. So even though it looks like a sports car on the outside, it's probably a submarine or something on the inside.

Once we've been waved past the gatehouse by a big, hairy hand, a bonfire-coloured eye crinkles in the driver's mirror. 'Excited to be back, Milly?'

I shrug and wriggle out of Max's gaze.

Truth is, I *am* excited. Excited to see my friends. Excited to dance again. My stomach is *pirouetting* all by itself.

'I've always wanted to meet the Captain,' says Leonora. 'He's my all-time hero.'

Max pretends to cough.

'You are too, Dad, but you've got to admit, the Captain's in a league of his own.' She wiggles around in her seat. 'Is it true that all his fingernails are missing, Milly?'

This is the nine hundred-and-ninety-ninth question about Swan House I've had to answer since Mum went away.

'Yes, the Captain's a *real* superhero,' I say, before going back to staring out of the window.

A fat dollop of rain splats on my nose and Leonora pulls up her velvety green hood.

'Looks like we got here just in time,' says Max, pressing a button. He talks to Leonora as the roof hums over my head. 'Actually, that reminds me, we had the lab results back from that umbrella you found. No fingerprints, but there were faint traces of gunpowder and something else the lab still hasn't identified. I'll keep you posted.'

At the end of the long driveway, a perfect white mansion comes into view – squeaky clean against the dirty sky.

'Anyway, here it is, Swan House School of Ballet. What do you think, Leo?'

'Wow,' says Leonora and my tummy flips. Is it

really only a few months since I saw Swan House for the first time too?

We pass a group of year eights in the car park. After everything that happened last term, I don't know whether to wave or hide, but Fleur and Danny grin and jog after us. Looks like I'm still in their good books. For now.

Max pulls up outside the entrance. I jump out and hold on to my beret as Leonora goggles at the stone pillars and marble swans.

'We've been looking out for you,' says Danny. He lowers his voice. 'Everyone's talking about the Scarlet Slippers. Wish I'd seen your fight with Filipp Pop—' His mouth drops open. 'Whoa. Is that who I think it is?'

Behind me, Max lifts my trunk from the boot.

Fleur's eyes almost pop out of her head. 'Max Deverall! OMG. I LOVE him. And who's that girl with him? What are they doing here? Milly, you've *got* to introduce us!'

I open my mouth and close it again. Danny's already shaking Max's hand. I catch the words 'biggest', and 'fan', and 'let me take your luggage'. It's like I've disappeared.

I grab my backpack and wander off in search of Lottie.

Rocking gently on the grass next to a crooked 'No

Parking' sign is a people carrier bouncing with kids. I skirt the door as it flings open and out tumble three identical chocolate-smeared children. A harrassed-looking woman tries to round them all up.

'Don't pull Saffy's hair, Archie. It's raining, Jemima, back in the car – what do you mean Gripper's escaped? ARCHIE BEE, DID YOU BRING THE HAMSTER?' Inside the car, a baby howls.

An older girl slides out of the front unnoticed. She crouches down and scoops something off the ground. 'Here, Archie.'

'MUM, MUM, I FOUND GRIPPER!' yells Archie.

'NO, LOOK AT ME, MUMMY! I'M DOING A TWIRL!'

'I'm going now, Mum,' says the older girl, turning around.

Yikes. It's my old roomie, Amy Bee – better known as Bumble. I duck behind a passing sixth former.

'Saffy, not in the puddle – not in the . . . Jemima? WHERE'S JEMIMA?'

Bumble pinches Archie's arm.

'OWWWW, Mum, AMY PINCHED ME!'

'Oh, Amy, what did you have to do that for? You off now, then, hun?' Bumble gets a quick peck on the cheek. 'JEMIMA, NOT NEAR THE LAKE!'

Saffy falls face-first into a puddle. Bumble picks her up, fastens her into a car seat, then watches her

Mum chase Jemima across the lawn. She shrugs on her backpack.

'See ya,' says Archie.

'Not if I see you first,' she says with a flick of curly brown hair.

I watch her make a beeline for Fleur. Judging by the golden glint in her eyes and the bounce in her curls, she's totally recovered from being poisoned last term. I puff a sigh of relief. I wouldn't wish death-by-poisoned-chocolate on anyone – even Willow Perkins's best friend.

Dipti Patel shouts 'hello' from the top of the school steps. I wave back. She looks shiny and new in her Christmas clothes – everyone does.

Well, almost everyone.

There's a boy puffing across the car park like Thomas the Tank Engine. His bushy, wet hair is bushier than ever. His bushy, wet monobrow is frowning like it's solving some impossible code, which it probably is. The same old padlocked satchel bounces across his shoulder and a white mask flaps around his neck. In his hand is a *Star Trek* thermos.

'Hi, Merv,' I say.

Merv looks up. 'Oh, it's you.'

That's Merv for 'hello'.

'How was your Christmas?' I ask.

'Good. Then bad. Then very bad.'

I wait for him to explain, but his monobrow does the talking – jiggling up and down in an incomprehensible Merv-like way.

Tyres screech behind us and I grab Merv's arm. Last term, Mrs Spencer almost flattened Merv before we'd even registered. This time it's Mr Spencer's turn.

Merv shakes me off as Benedict Spencer flings open the car door and jumps out. He's wearing a puffy, black ski jacket and expensive black trainers. They're exactly like the ones he had last term, only newer.

Spencer has a white mark on his face in the shape of a pair of ski goggles. He's probably spent the Christmas holidays snowboarding or sledging, or doing some other snowy pursuit beginning with 's'.

He checks out my high-tops. 'What happened to your shoes, Milky Bar?'

Milky Bar?

'See what I did there, Kydd?'

I groan at the joke while Spencer drags an enormous trunk on to the road. He glances at Merv's shabby old suitcase. 'Thought you weren't going home for Christmas.'

Merv grunts. 'Ms Celia wouldn't let me stay in school. Had to go back to Ray's flat.'

'Who's Ray?' asks Spencer as his dad zooms away.

Merv grunts and hugs his thermos.

'He's Merv's mum's boyfriend.' I explain. 'I bet she was really pleased to see you, Merv.'

'She wasn't there. That was the good part. She and Ray'd gone away.'

'Gone away – where?'

Merv's monobrow slumps. 'Vegas. Elvis married them on Christmas Day.'

I think about Mum and Max and my shoulders slump too. 'Sorry, Merv.'

'That wasn't the worst part. They auctioned my *Star Trek* collection to pay for the flights.' Merv hrumphs. 'It wasn't even the real Elvis. They sold my nineteen sixty-seven Type One Phaser to get hitched by a Welshman called Bryn.'

If Merv was like other people, I'd give him a hug. Even Spencer's lost for words.

Unfortunately, it doesn't take him long to find them again. 'Never mind, Merv. You've still got an intergalactic thermos.'

Across the driveway, I spot a small, black-haired girl climbing out of a battered brown car.

I shout out. 'Lottie, over here!'

'MILLYYYYY!'

Lottie hurdles a line of suitcases and barrels into Spencer.

'Steady, Shorty!'

She thumps Spencer on the arm and turns her

dimply grin on me. There's still a gap where one of her front teeth should be.

'Lottie – your tooth?' I say. 'I thought you were going to the dentist in the holidays.'

'I did,' grins Lottie, 'but he only went an' banned me for life. Never meant to hurt him, but you should've seen his needle. I hate flamin' needles.' She shudders. 'Anyhow, I told my mum and dad all about you – not everyfink, but you know what I mean – and they want to say hello.'

Mr and Mrs Li trundle over with Lottie's bags. Lottie's mum nudges her dad. 'Sai, this is Lottie's friend what won the Scarlet Slipper.' She brushes a stray ginger curl from her eyes. 'Well done, sausage. I keep tellin' Lott she ain't cut out for ballet, but she don't listen, do she, Sai?'

Mr Li winks at me. 'Lottie's just like her mother. She's got her temper too – I blame the red hair.'

Mrs Li punches his arm.

'You see, Milly,' he says, 'it's like living with two lionesses.'

Mrs Li snorts. 'S'pose you fink that makes you a lion.'

'OK, you two,' says Lottie. 'You've met Milly, so you can go now.'

Mrs Li catches her hand. 'Not before I've 'ad a cuddle.'

Lottie squirms out of her mum's hold. She's so lucky. Thanks to Max Deverall, my mum could be anywhere right now.

'You look like you need a cuddle too, poppet.' Mrs Li wraps me in her arms. Her coat's a bit scratchy but I don't mind. She smells like Lottie – of peppermint shampoo and pluck.

'Bye, then,' says Lottie, dragging me towards the school. 'See you at half-term and no arguin' while I'm away.'

'Wait,' calls Mr Li. 'You forgot your arnica.' He gives her a little jar of ointment. 'It's the best thing for bruises.'

Lottie kisses her dad's cheek. 'Fanks, Dad.'

As we run to catch up with the boys, she asks me about my bad ankle.

'It's fine,' I say. 'I can't wait to start dancing again.'

Lottie pauses at the bottom of the steps. 'Yeah, and I can't wait for Spy Craft wiv the Captain. Look, there he is.'

Framed in one the windows, a Viking god peers across the lawn. The Captain tugs his ponytail beard and turns away.

'Looks like someone got out on the wrong side of bed this mornin',' says Lottie. 'Do you fink somefink's up?'

The last time I saw the Captain tug his beard was when Filipp Popov poisoned Bumble. What if the Mouse King's struck again? I wish I could talk to Lottie about him but Mum made me promise. I blink up at the stormy sky and say a prayer to the Viking gods.

Please, please, send her home soon.

7

A New Mentor

There's a loud sneeze from the entrance. A tall, gangly woman ushers us into the hall. She has a bright-pink bobble hat and a nose to match. 'Happy New Year, swanlets!'

'Happy New Year, Topsy,' I say. 'Are you OK?'

She trumpets into a spotty pink hankie. '*Be?* What do you bean? I'b as fit as a fiddle! If I was ill or infectious or anythig, I wouldn't be here, *obvs*. Bizz Celia would have found sub super clever, totally qualified person to take over as your housebisstress and I'd be out on the street.' Topsy sniffs. 'Hurry up, Berv, it's cold out there. You'll catch your death.'

Merv pulls his mask over his nose.

'S'all right, Topsy,' says Lottie. 'If *you* left, your mum'd go wiv you, and what would we eat then?'

'Real food?' says Spencer, popping a stick of gum in his mouth.

Topsy lifts the flap of her bobble hat. 'What was

that, Spencer? Can't hear a thig. Now, there was subthig I was suppose to tell you. What was it?'

Merv mumbles through his mask. 'We'vegottogostraighttothetheatre.'

'What did he say? Ooo, I rebeber, you've got to go straight to the theatre. Bizz Celia's waitig with sub super excitig news. By lips are sealed, but it's about Badab leavig all of a sudden. And a VERY fabous person takig her place. Can't say any more than that except –' Topsy does a little hop and flaps her arms like a woolly, pink ostrich – 'our new Head of Ballet is BAX DEVERALL!'

Drat. I've been so happy to see everyone, I'd forgotten about the Deveralls.

'Flamin' Nora, I never knew Max Deverall was a spy,' says Lottie.

Merv follows us into the lobby and pulls down his mask. 'That's because it's top secret. He and his daughter have been undercover for years.'

'Never knew he had a daughter neiver,' says Lottie.

'Her name's Leonora.' Merv's monobrow sighs. 'I met her once when I was eight and three-quarters. We were both FT'd.'

'FT'd?' I say, touching Dame Anna Popova's little statue for luck. 'Merv, I wish you'd speak one of the five languages I do understand.'

'*Fast-tracked*,' says Merv, in his do-I-have-to-explain-everything voice. 'Leonora has an IQ of a hundred and forty-nine.'

Of course she has. Leonora Deverall the wonderkid.

Lottie sniffs. 'Urgh. What's that stink?'

'It's coming from the refectory,' says Spencer. 'Smells like Cook's stewing pondweed for lunch.'

Outside the theatre, a little group of year sevens are huddled around Jada Gayle, the head girl. One of them spots me and asks for my autograph. Spencer tells her not to be such a toady and gives her his instead.

'Hello, Milly,' says Jada. My cheeks go hot. The coolest girl in school was on a top secret mission last term. She's never spoken to me before. 'Glad I caught you – I've got a message from Dafydd.'

My cheeks go hotter. The head boy rehearsed with me last term. Bab would say he's to *diiie* for.

'He said to say congratulations, you did us proud, girl.' She tucks a corkscrew curl behind her ear.

'Where is he?' I ask.

'Haven't you heard? He broke his shoulder skiing. He'll be out of action for months.'

My stomach sinks like Cook's Victoria sponge.

'Anyway, I've got your updated Swanphones here. The Captain says to put them on straight away. And *you*,' she says, scowling at Spencer. 'Lose the gum if you don't want a detention. Hurry up, assembly's about to start.' She shoos us away with long, dark fingers.

I sigh. 'There's more grace in Jada's little finger than there is in my entire being.'

Lottie bends her Swanphone around her wrist. 'Cheer up, Milly, Madge made Dafydd's avatar last term. Maybe he'll turn up as someone's mentor.' She nudges me in the ribs. 'I bet you anyfink they'll give you a nice new mentor now they know how Filipp turned out. You never know, you and Dafydd might get paired togever.'

I hope Lottie's right. I know he was still a schoolboy when they made his avatar, but I'd rather eat poisoned chocolate than see Filipp Popov again.

In the theatre, rain pit-pats against the windows. The screen onstage lights up with the school badge – a pair of swans and the school motto: *Cycni venustas, cor leonis. Grace of a swan, heart of a lion.*

Leonora glides past with Fleur. With her perfect posture and elegant top-knot, she already looks totally at home.

The side of the stage creaks as the Captain shifts from foot to foot. Waiting in his Thor-shaped shadow, eyes as flickery as ever, is Max Deverall.

Spencer points down the aisle. 'Is that Leonora Deverall?'

'Where?' asks Merv, craning his neck like a one-eyebrowed meerkat.

'The girl in green, sitting next to Fleur Fontaine. Looks like the Fairy of the Woodland Glade.'

I look across the hall and catch Leonora's eye.

'Over here, Milly,' she calls. 'I saved you a seat.' There's that familiar smile again.

'It's OK,' I mouth back. 'I'm with my friends.'

'I'LL GO!' says Merv with un-Merv-like enthusiasm. I watch as he shuffles towards Leonora at un-Merv-like speed.

Traitor.

'You'd think we weren't brainy enough for him,' says Spencer. 'How do you know Leonora, Milky Bar?'

I'm halfway through explaining about my tragically ruined Christmas when Ms Celia marches on to the stage like she has somewhere else she needs to be. In fact, our director doesn't look like she had a very merry Christmas either. Underneath her green paisley scarf, her forehead is as sharply creased as her trousers.

She plants her hands deep in her pockets and the theatre falls silent. Ms Celia has the same effect on everyone. She can shut you up, push back your shoulders and make you ten centimetres taller just by looking at you. She can also make you ten centimetres smaller.

'Welcome back to Swan House,' she says in her no-nonsense voice. 'Before I discuss the coming term, I have some announcements to make. First, I'm sorry to report that our head boy, Dafydd Wynn-Jones, was involved in a skiing accident over the holidays. He is making good progress but unfortunately his time as a student at Swan House has come to an end. Therefore I've asked William Flynn to take his place.'

William Flynn's friends give a limp, half-hearted sort of cheer. Everyone knows no one can replace Dafydd.

'Second, most of you are aware that following a rather disagreeable turn of events, Madame de La Cloche is no longer with us.'

This time the cheer in the theatre is noisily whole-hearted. Mine and Lottie's are possible the loudest and definitely the longest. Ms Celia's forehead creases in our direction and we stop cheering imme-diately.

'AS I WAS SAYING . . . I have appointed a new Head of Ballet – a gentleman whose talents reach far beyond the world of dance. Girls and boys, we are extremely lucky to welcome to Swan House, Mr Max Deverall.'

Everyone at the back squirms to get a better view. Max, smooth as a new satin ballet shoe, steps out of the Captain's shadow and flashes his superstar smile.

'Thank you, Ms Celia. I'm excited to be here. But everyone, please just call me Max.'

I roll my eyes and clap as quietly as possible. 'Honestly,' I say to Lottie, 'I don't know what all the fuss is about.'

Ms Celia signals for quiet. 'Max's arrival is extremely timely. Due to our triumph at the Scarlet Slippers, Swan House has come to the attention of the Dance Schools Inspectorate. They have decided, most inconveniently, to carry out an inspection.'

The Captain rumbles like a faraway storm. 'Of course,' continues Ms Celia, 'none of the inspectors are aware of the work we do at Swan House, so I urge each and every one of you to be on your guard. I have asked Max to choose this term's programme with the inspection in mind.'

Max nods. 'I know it's an unusual choice for this time of year, but I thought we'd start with *The Nutcracker*. It'll mean the fencing classes scheduled for this term can continue under the guise of the battle scene in Act One. Plus, *The Nutcracker* has it all – ensemble pieces, character dances, great solos – everyone will have a part to play.'

My heart does a hop and a skip. I've always wanted to dance the Sugar Plum Fairy.

Lottie whispers in my ear. 'Sugar Plum was one of Nora's solos. She can help us rehearse.'

I give her an under-the-chair fist bump. Lottie's mentor is a brilliant teacher – in fact she's brilliant at everything.

'Thank you, Max,' says Ms Celia with a nod that pushes him back in the Captain's shadow. 'And finally, I would like to take a moment to honour four students without whom we would not be here today.' Her gaze softens. 'Please join me in thanking Benedict Spencer, Lottie Li, Merv Crump and Milly Kydd for the enormous courage they showed last term. And special congratulations to Milly, who brought the Scarlet Slipper back to Swan House.'

There's a *hurrah* and Danny stands up. Sugar Plum Fairies! They're all standing up. Spencer takes a bow. Lottie punches my arm. The hoots and applause make my heart fill up like a hot-water bottle cat. I wish Mum was here to hear them.

On the screen behind Ms Celia, the pair of swans morph into a lion's head and its roar welcomes us back. *Cycni venustas, cor leonis!*

I try to follow Spencer as he swaggers down the aisle, but I can't move for backslaps, well done's and way-to-go's.

Another hand pats my shoulder, but this one holds on and yanks me to one side.

'Millicent Kydd, the heroine of the hour,' says a girl with a mouth that goes down in the corners.

'Hello, Bumble,' I say. 'I'm glad you're feeling better.'

'Don't pretend you're happy to see me back. Everyone else might have forgotten what happened last term, but I haven't. We both know you left that chocolate out on purpose.'

'Don't be silly, Bumble. I didn't even know it was poisoned. It came from Filipp Popov.'

I try to shake her off but she pulls me into a fake hug and hisses breath and spite in my ear.

'Get this into your stupid little skull: Ms Celia might have given you all the solos last term, but if I don't get the Sugar Plum Fairy, I'll make sure you're the one who ends up in the infirmary.'

A voice booms from the hall. 'Move it, you two. You can kiss and make up later. Everyone apart from Deverall, Spencer and Kydd, take your cases to your dorms. You three, follow us.'

I stumble out of the theatre, away from Bumble with her poison breath and scorchy eyes, and chase after the others.

The Captain is already on the grand staircase, taking the stairs four at a time. By the time I catch up with him, I'm completely out of puff.

'In here,' he says, pointing at a classroom opposite the gym. 'This is our new classroom until the inspector's done.' He points at the chairs. 'Take a pew.'

I plop down and puff as quietly as possible. Spencer asks if I need to lie down.

Obviously not quietly enough.

The Captain shrugs off his jacket and rolls each of his shirt sleeves over a muscly forearm. 'Deverall, I assume you've been issued with a new Swanphone?'

Leonora drags her eyes away from the Captain's puckered fingertips. 'Yes, Captain.'

'Good. You'll need it to enter most areas of the school and to activate your mentor. Has anyone briefed you about the MNTR program yet?'

'Yes,' says Leonora. 'My dad said everyone at Swan House has a virtual mentor to help with their studies. He said they're all avatars of past students.'

'That's right, pet.' The Captain loosens his tie and tucks it in his pocket. 'Making avatars is one of the Shoe Keeper's jobs. You'll meet Madge Little soon enough.'

'That's really cool,' says Leonora slowly, 'but Captain, my dad's been my mentor since I was five years old. I don't need a virtual one.'

The Captain scratches his hairy jaw. 'Just because you've worked in the field doesn't mean you don't need a mentor. Believe us, it could save your *derrière* one day.'

I mutter to Spencer. 'My mentor wouldn't save anyone's *derrière*. In fact, he's been a total pain in mine from the start.'

Leonora nods patiently. 'With respect, Captain, my dad's got ten times more experience than any of the students here – past or present.'

'That might be true, but you're forgetting something,' says the Captain. 'Your da's got more than one person to look out for at Swan House. The fact is, you've *all* been paired with a new mentor.'

'Me too? A new mentor?' My heart pitter-patters a name. *Dafydd Wynn-Jones. Dafydd Wynn-Jones.*

Spencer yawns and stretches his legs. 'I don't get it. What do I need a new mentor for?'

'After our brush with Korolev and his dance academy last term, we thought you might want someone on the right side of the law.'

Leonora raises an eyebrow. 'Ivan Korolev's your mentor?'

Spencer shrugs. 'Korolev's school trains the deadliest kids in lycra, so what? His avatar was made before he was expelled from Swan House. Besides, I quite like the little weasel.'

'I thought you might say that,' says the Captain. 'It's your choice, but Crump noticed a few irregularities with Ivan last term. Any funny business and you're to report it to us, pronto. Got it?'

'Got it,' says Spencer.

The Captain's ponytail beard swings over to me.

'You don't want to keep Popov, do you, Kydd?'

'No, Captain!'

'Good. Let's hope you're luckier this time around. Ready, pet?'

I cross everything I can without falling off my chair and ask my Swanphone to activate my new mentor. Seconds later, a ghostly shape appears in front of me. Its friendly grin hangs in the air like a see-through Cheshire cat.

I hold my breath and wait for the rest of the boy to snap into focus.

I'm quite dizzy by the time my new mentor offers me a chubby, virtual hand.

'Greetings, Milly,' he says. 'Delighted to meet you. My name is Trevor Topping.'

8

Trevor, as in Topping

My mouth drops open. 'Topping, as in Topsy? Topping, as in Cook?'

Uh-oh. Topping, as in *dead as a doornail*.

'One and the same,' says the Captain.

Spencer snorts with barely disguised glee.

My new mentor has a short neck, stumpy legs and round, pink cheeks. He looks like he's spent the last thirty-five years squashed inside one of Cook's pickling jars. Crushed, I try to beam back.

'It's an honour to be paired with you, Milly, an honour. Never won a Scarlet Slipper trophy myself, but it's never too late, is it? Rule Five of *The Guide to Espionage* – Try, try, and try again. That's the Topping motto.'

Trevor's voice is as cheery as a cherry on top of a cake. I haven't the heart to tell him it is too late. Waaay.

'Now what can I help you w—' Trevor starts to

dim. He crackles and pops, then with an apologetic grin, he disappears into nothing.

I frown at the Captain. 'I didn't tell my Swanphone to switch him off. What happened?'

'Sorry, pet, Topping's avatar was an early prototype. Come to think of it, it might even have been the first avatar the old Shoe Keeper made. As far as I know he's never been paired with anyone before. He can't have been the sharpest pencil in the case. Deverall, let's hope you've got someone with a bit more nous.'

Seconds later, we're joined by a boy with a nice, normal neck, long, muscly legs and cheekbones you could sharpen a pencil with. If it wasn't for the faintest glow, he'd look discombobulatingly real.

I cross my arms. I let out a *huff*. I even do a little stomp.

'Hello, Leonora,' says Dafydd Wynn-Jones's avatar. 'Welcome to Swan House.'

The Captain's straw-coloured eyebrows meet in the middle. 'Don't blame us, pet. The MNTR program's a bliddy mystery to us.'

I can't take my eyes off Dafydd. 'He looks almost real!'

'Aye, Madge started upgrading the avatars over Christmas.' The Captain checks his Swanphone. 'Right, I'll see you all in Spy Craft tomorrow.

One thirty sharp. Remember to watch out for the inspector!'

We all get up to leave.

'Spencer,' calls the Captain. 'Haven't you forgotten something?'

Spencer trundles back to his seat and unpeels his gum from under the chair. He winks at me.

'Bring it here.' The Captain stretches the gum between his fingers and pulls something from it.

'If I ever catch you smuggling a listening device into my room again, I will personally *fast*-track you into year four,' he says. 'Ill-advised but well executed – now get out of my sight.'

I stomp down the stairs. Away from the Captain. *Stomp.*

Away from Spencer's smirk. *Stomp, stomp.*

Away from Leonora and Dafydd. *Stomp, stomp, stomp.*

It's like the worst kind of déjà vu. First I get paired with Filipp Popov and now Trevor Topping. It's SO unfair.

Leonora calls out. 'Are you going for lunch, Milly?'

My 'No' is drowned out by the small mob waiting in the hall.

'There she is!' says Dipti Patel.

I brace myself for more back slaps and 'way-to-gos', but Dipti runs right past me and practically curtsies to Leonora. 'You're going to *love* Swan House!'

'Is Dafydd your mentor?' gushes Fleur, gawping at his avatar. 'I hope they put you in our dorm.'

A voice like a wasp sting interrupts. 'I thought I was in your dorm this term, Fleur.' Bumble glares up from the bottom of the stairs. 'You can't expect me to share with her again. If it wasn't for Milly, I wouldn't have spent half of last term throwing my guts up.'

'Ew, Bumble, can we not talk about that again,' says Fleur, wrinkling her cute little nose.

Bumble's eyes flash from me to Fleur. 'I had a temperature of forty degrees!'

I'd like to point out that her temperature would have been perfectly normal if she hadn't eaten my chocolate in the first place, but I don't get a chance. Trevor chooses that very moment to reappear.

'Who's that?'

I switch him off. 'No one.'

'I recognize him from the Hall of Fame. It was Trevor Topping, wasn't it? OMG. Milly's been paired with the World's Worst Spy. It's the perfect match.'

Bumble's upside-down smile makes me wish I could disappear into thin air too.

'Ignore her. Come and get some pondweed,' says Spencer, heading for the refectory.

'You go, Spence. I'll see you there.'

I plod to the loos. I wouldn't feel so bad if Bumble wasn't right. The MNTR program's paired me with the World's Worst Spy. What does that say about me?

If I had a ponytail beard, I'd pull it right out.

'Billy, wait!' pants a voice behind me.

I plod faster. I really can't face any more Toppings today.

Topsy lollops after me. 'Is it true, Billy?' she calls.

'Is what true?'

'I just heard Fleur tellig Danny that Daddy's your new mentor – they seebed very jolly about it.'

It takes me a moment to translate what she's saying.

Topsy claps her hands. 'It's tooo excitig! He's never been used before. Do you think I could take the tiniest peek?'

Topsy's face is all pink and expectant. I stop plodding and make sure no one can see us. 'I suppose so.'

Trevor flickers into focus. 'Greetings, Milly. What can I do for you?'

Topsy bobs around her dad's avatar in delight. 'THANK YOU, BILLY! Oooooo-er.'

She stops hopping and squints into his slightly spotty face.

'Sorry, Topsy, this must be a bit strange for you.'

'It is a bit.' Topsy rubs her eyes. 'But are you sure it's hib?'

75

'Definitely. Why?'

'I never saw hib when he was a teenager, *obvs*, but I'b certain-sure he had brown eyes.'

I hadn't noticed much beyond Trevor's beaming smile. I'm a little surprised when my stare is met with a pair of cat-green eyes.

'Perhaps the Shoe Keeper bade a bistake. I'll ask Bubby. She always says he was handsub. He is handsub, isn't he?'

Somewhere down the corridor, a door closes and footsteps echo towards us. I glance over my shoulder. Jada Gayle and William Flynn are coming this way. 'Er, yes, *very*. Do you mind if I switch him off now?'

Topsy backs away. 'Course not. Sorry to take up your lunch hour. You'd better get to the refectory before everyone polishes off Bubby's sherry and spinach trifle.'

She smiles and I get the biggest twang of guilt for thinking mean things about her dad.

Suppose the least I can do is to force down her mum's food.

Spencer dangles something from his fork and starts to chew. 'Frog's legs. When Cook said this was Toad in the Hole, I should have known she meant *literally*.'

Lottie tucks a napkin under her dimply chin. 'It's your own fault. Told you to have the egg sarnies. So what did the Captain want, Milly?'

I pick the shell out of my sandwich while I tell her about my new mentor.

She frowns. 'I don't get it. Why's the program paired you wiv Trevor Toppin'?'

'I don't know. Even the Captain said he was useless.'

Spencer moves on to his spinach trifle. 'Should have seen Kydd's face when Deverall got Wynn-Jones.'

Lottie ignores him. 'Maybe Trevor's got hidden talents?'

'I hope not,' I say. 'My last mentor had "hidden talents" and look where that got me.'

I put down my eggshell sandwich and silently apologize to Topsy. I did try. Just as well I've got a term's supply of *kozulya* in my trunk.

As I push away my plate, my Swanphone begins to flash. 'Ooo, the dorms have been posted.'

'Look,' says Lottie, waving her wrist under my nose. 'We're sharin', Milly.'

There's a picture of three faces on my Swanphone. Mine, Lottie's and . . . *drat*.

'What's wrong?' asks Lottie.

'Nothing, it's just Leonora Deverall's in with us too. She's so—' I search for the word.

'Borin'?' says Lottie.

'No.'

'Big-headed?' says Lottie.

'No.'

'Bossy?' says Lottie.

'No.'

'What, then?'

I slump. 'Perfect.'

'She seemed all right to me,' says Spencer.

'You didn't have to spend Christmas with her.'

In the picture Leonora's smiling that smile again. Who does she look like? It's on the feathery edges of my memory when a second message appears on my phone. I forget all about Leonora and jump up from the table.

'Where are you goin'?' asks Lottie.

I do a little skip. 'To see Mr Stubbs!'

9

Tea with Mr Stubbs

I find Ms Celia talking with Max outside the coach house. Max's sports car gleams next to Ms Celia's Morris Minor, Winifred. The sun's out even though it's still raining. I search for a rainbow but all I spot is Fleur and Dipti giggling under the arch. I roll my eyes – the Deluded Deverall Fan Club.

'Hello, Milly,' says Ms Celia. 'Is your ankle better now?'

I go up on my *demi pointes*. 'Much better, thanks, Ms Celia.'

'I'm very pleased to hear it. As I said in my message, Mrs Huntley-Palmer called to say that Heart Maker is in Meekes today. He's not back at work yet, you understand, but she asked if you'd like to see him. Given that we don't start classes until tomorrow, I said yes.'

All the shoemakers at Meekes are named after the

little symbol they stamp on their shoes. Mr Stubbs's heart suits him perfectly. I stop myself from skipping again. Ms Celia doesn't approve of frivolous skipping on just-healed ankles.

'Max is going to collect an order for Leonora. You don't mind taking Milly, do you, Max?' She doesn't wait for an answer. 'Excellent. Send him my best wishes.'

The bell tinkles as we step through Meekes's shiny red door. Mrs Huntley-Palmer looks up and the shoe-box in her hand spills on to the whirly red carpet.

'Heavens, Mr Deverall – what a treat! Come in, come in.'

'Max, please, Dorothy,' says Max, his eyes zooming from the old-fashioned desk, to the staircase, to the exit at the back of the shop. 'The old place has hardly changed. And neither have you.'

I roll my eyes again. Max is as smooth and oozy as a chocolate fountain.

Mrs H-P pats her hair. Today it's winding round and round and up and up like a Ho-Ho-Helterskelter. 'What can we do for you? Can I get you a cup of tea? A digestive biscuit? I've got some Viennese whirls in the back office.'

'That sounds great, but I'll have to take a rain check.'

Max whispers in Mrs H-P's ear and her small hands flutter over her heart.

'So you see, I've got to pop out. Would you mind seeing to Milly?'

I frown. We've only just got here.

'Who?' Mrs H-P seems to have forgotten all about me. 'Oh yes! Heart Maker is downstairs, dear. He's still recuperating, and I thought a visit from you might cheer him up.'

The staircase is as rickety as ever, but at least someone's put in a solid new handrail. Poor Mr Stubbs didn't stand a chance when Filipp Popov pushed him down the stairs.

I pass his old workbench and a chill trickles down my neck.

Across the room I spot a pair of excessively shaggy eyebrows in a kindly old face. Mr Stubbs is perched on a stool next to his bench. Propped against it is a walking stick. He's wearing the woolly Christmas tank top Mrs Stubbs knitted last year. He looks thinner without his apron and his face is all hollows and wrinkles, but I'm relieved to see the same bright twinkle in his china-blue eyes.

'Miss Millicent! Well, I never. Look, lads! It's the winner of the Scarlet Slipper 'erself. Didn't I always say she'd do it?'

The shoemakers crowd around me. 'He did too,' says Diamond Maker.

Star Maker shakes my hand. 'Well done, Miss.'

I smile. 'How are you feeling, Mr Stubbs?'

'I'm tickety-boo, miss. Tickety-boo. My knees ain't quite what they used to be, but I'm still standin'.' His hand shakes as he reaches for his stick. 'Did anyone tell you what 'appened, miss?'

I nod. 'I'm so sorry. It must have been a horrible shock.'

Mr Stubbs nods sadly. 'I don't know what came over the lad, miss. He must 'ave 'ad a bit of a turn.'

'Alf treated him like a son, he did,' tuts Star Maker. 'Lucky he's a tough old boot.'

Mr Stubbs wipes an eye. 'I don't know about that, Scarpelli. Me knees'll get better soon enough but I don't think me old ticker'll ever get over it.'

Anger sparks inside me. How could Filipp have hurt such a kindly old man?

Diamond Maker growls. 'If I ever get my 'ands on the little toe-rag—'

Mr Stubbs holds up a trembly hand. 'Now, now, Bert, ladies present. I just made a pot of Rosie Lee, miss. Why don't you take the weight off your plates and tell me about your mum.'

Over the hum of sewing machines, I tell Mr Stubbs

about Mum's 'amnesia' and score myself a one out of ten on the fib-o-meter. Lying to Mr Stubbs is ten times harder than lying to Willow Perkins.

'That's music to me shell-likes, miss. I expect she'll be at 'ome for a while to get over it.'

'No, she's away again. Touring, you know . . .'

My voice wavers.

'I see,' says Mr Stubbs, giving me a biscuit. 'And did I just 'ear 'Er Upstairs say 'ello to Max Deverall?'

'Yes. He's taken over from Madame as our new Head of Ballet.'

''As 'e now?'

Mr Stubbs scoops three spoonfuls of sugar into his tea and gives it an absent-minded stir. 'I remember Master Max when 'e was at school. Used to come 'ere with your mum and a few other lads. Terrors they was too – don't know 'ow your mum put up with all their antics.'

I put down my mug. 'You knew Max Deverall?'

'I did an' all. Back when Edwina Meekes was runnin' the shop an' I still 'ad me own teeth. Young Ivan and Max Deverall was as thick as tea leaves.' Mr Stubbs sucks his teeth like he's checking they're still there. 'Funny ole world, ain't it? One minute, Master Ivan's disappeared off the planet. And the next, 'is ballet school's turned up in the Scarlet Slippers.'

There's a warble from upstairs. 'Milly, dear, Mr Deverall's back.'

I put down my mug. 'Sorry, Mr Stubbs, I've got to go. Don't get up, I'll see you again soon.'

Mr Stubbs pats my hand. 'Reckon you'll have fun with your new 'ead of Ballet, Miss. A right joker 'e was back in the day, and if it's true what thay say about jokers – they don't ever change their spots.'

10

Leonora's Little Secret

After supper that evening, Spencer asks if we want to play a virtual reality flight-simulation game he got for Christmas.

I've never seen Merv's monobrow look so excited. 'I don't understand why you don't want to play,' he says. 'It sold out online in three and a half seconds!'

The thought of a 'virtual reality flight-simulation game' makes me want to throw myself out of a plane without a parachute. And anyway, I've got other things on my mind. Where did Max Deverall slope off to today? He was super-cagey in the car on the way back. When I asked him where he'd been he started whistling the same old soppy tune from *Romeo and Juliet*.

Lottie yawns. 'Sorry, Spence, I'm goin' to the dorm. I'm done in an' I ain't even unpacked yet. You comin', Milly?'

As we step out into the drizzle, I mull over

everything Mr Stubbs said about Max and Ivan Korolev.

Lottie hooks her arm through mine. 'Everyfink all right, Milly? You ain't said much since you got back from Meekes.'

'Sorry. I just was just thinking about Max Deverall.'

'What about him?'

'I just wish we had some other teacher.'

'Why? Max'll be a million times better than Madame! I'm almost lookin' forward to ballet wivout her pickin' on us every five minutes. '

'Max thinks he's a million times better than everyone. And Leonora's just the same. They're like superheroes.'

I sigh. The only good thing about him being in school is he isn't with Mum.

We reach Ms Celia's coach house and pass under the arch. Rain drips from the woody tangle of wisteria and trickles down my neck. 'Actually, Lottie, when I was in Meekes today, it was really strange, Max—'

'Uh-oh,' interrupts Lottie. 'Don't look now – courtyard, twelve o'clock. It's Supergirl.'

On the path in front of us, Leonora's red and gold highlights gleam under the carriage lights. She moves along the path as if she's floating. Her feet don't make a sound.

I pull Lottie back but it's too late – I'd forgotten Leonora was half owl.

She whirls around. 'Oh, it's you, Milly. And you must be Lottie. I've heard so much about you.'

Lottie juts out her dimply chin. 'Yeah and it's all true, so you'd better watch out if you know what's good for you.'

Leonora smiles like she thinks Lottie's joking.

'I'm so glad I'm in your dorm. I'm sure that Bumble girl would have never forgiven me if I'd ended up sharing with Fleur and Dipti.'

'She'll hate you anyway,' says Lottie. 'She reckoned she'd be Queen Bee around here now that Willow's gone to Hollywood, but you've shown up and stolen her crown.'

Leonora laughs. 'It won't take her long to realize I'm not a queen bee – I'm not a queen anything.'

In front of us, the old stables make the shape of a half-moon in the darkness. Leonora points at the light glowing from behind each little shuttered window. 'Wow. Are these the dorms? They look so old. You can almost hear the horses' hooves.'

'Nah,' says Lottie. 'It's just Topsy in her unicorn onesie.'

Leonora laughs again. 'So who used to live here?'

'The Astus family,' says Lottie. 'The last Lord

Astus had rooms over the feartre until he snuffed it. But that was yonks ago.'

She opens our dorm door and Leonora's face lights up. 'Oh, I wasn't expecting it be homely! The sleighbeds are so cute, and I love the clouds on the ceiling. Do you mind if I sleep nearest the door?'

'Fine with me if I can have the bed *furthest* from the door,' I say.

Lottie shrugs and throws her suitcase on the bed in the middle. She scoops up an armful of clothes and chucks them in her cupboard in a big, messy heap. I put my hot-water bottle Boris on my pillow, then search through my trunk for my pyjamas and washbag. The rest can wait until tomorrow.

Leonora takes *aaaaages* to put her things away. 'I like being organized,' she says. 'Guess I'm used to leaving places in a hurry.'

Lottie climbs into bed and catches my eye. Her eyebrows say, *I see what you mean*. Her lips say, 'Get a move on, Leonora. It'll be time to get up again soon.'

Leonora lays her hoody on the bed and starts to fold. 'Sorry, I'm trained to get by without much sleep.'

Lottie gives her pillow a thump. 'Well I ain't and I want to be awake in your dad's class tomorrow.'

'It's going to be so cool. Have you danced *The Nutcracker* before, Lottie?'

'Nah, but Nora Doone's danced the Sugar Plum Fairy loads of times and she's the best.'

Leonora stops folding and seems to forget all about being organized. 'Actually, Lottie, there's something I've got to tell you. About your mentor, I mean.'

Lottie's dimples vanish. 'If you've got anyfink bad to say about Nora, I'll knock your block off.'

'It's nothing like that.' Leonora takes the longest, deepest breath, like she's about to dive in the lake.

'Well? What is it?' I say with a yawn.

'Nora Doone's my mom.'

Lottie's mouth drops open. 'Your what?'

My hot-water bottle Boris thuds to the floor.

Nora Doone. That's who Leonora reminds me of. Why didn't I see it before? Even her name is a clue. Leo*nora*.

Leonora's explanation comes out in a big gush. 'Eva told me Mum was a mentor here in the Christmas holidays.'

'Mum told you?' I say in a small voice. Why didn't she tell *me*? And how many more surprise parents are going to pop up in Swan House this term? First Trevor and now Nora, who next? It's very discombobulating.

'I think she and dad were worried that it would upset me – you know, seeing her in school every day. But I really want to meet her avatar, and it's great that she's still able to help the kids here. Dad says it's what she would've wanted.'

Her eyes have gone all melty and even though I don't want it to, my heart goes melty too.

Lottie starts bouncing on her bed. 'That's SOOO COOL! Nora's a LEGEND! You can see her right now if you like?'

She doesn't wait for Leonora to answer. Before you can say 'Lilac fairy', Nora Doone is arranging herself at the end of Lottie's bed. She unruffles her lilac tutu and smooths the flowers in her honey hair.

My eyes go from Leonora to Nora and back again. As well as her smile, Leonora has her mum's poise and grace.

'Hello, Lottie,' says Nora. 'Welcome back to Swan House. What can I do for you?'

'I want you to meet someone,' replies Lottie. 'She's new to Swan House.'

Nora gazes at Leonora. 'My program was updated this morning. You're Leonora Isabel Deverall. Welcome.'

Leonora's eyes are as big and watery as the puddles outside. 'Thanks, Nora. It's nice to meet you.'

'Listen up, Nora, Leonora's got somefink to tell you.' Lottie pats her bed. 'You can sit next to her if you like, Leonora.'

Leonora shakes her head. 'It's OK, Lottie. Her avatar is just a schoolgirl. Eva warned me that she wouldn't get who I am.' She puts her hand through her virtual mum's. 'I'm just happy she's here.'

I swing my legs out of bed and dig my toes into the rug. Neither of them notice me going to the bathroom.

I plonk myself on the loo seat and stare at the mirror. Lottie worships Nora and now she's going to worship her daughter too. It's so unfair. First Max takes Mum away and now Leonora is trying to take Lottie. My face is blotched and ugly, but not half as ugly as the things I'd like to say to Leonora Deverall.

My Swanphone flashes red. 'Alert. Your heart rate and rise in blood pressure would indicate a high level of stress. Please breathe deeply through your nose and out through your mouth or visit Nurse for further advice.'

I turn my Swanphone off. Nurse can't give me the kind of advice I need.

How can anyone compete with Supergirl?

11

The Fencing Lesson

I breathe in the smell of the dance studio – wood polish, perspiration, rosin. It whisks me back like a like a twirling time machine – back to Madame's sharp tongue, back to Willow's bullying, back to Ballet Tots and never quite feeling good enough.

But this term is going to be different.

After dipping my shoes in the rosin tray, I join Lottie and Leonora at the barre. They're talking about all the times Nora saved the world. I suppose it runs in the family.

Leonora whispers something in Lottie's ear. She guffaws over the rain drumming noisily against the windows. The door opens and Lottie looks up, but it's only our pianist, Miss Batty. Her soggy brown cardigan hangs below her knees. Her woolly tights are wrinkled around her ankles. She looks like she's swum across the lake to get here. She scurries to the piano, leaving behind a trail of slippery, wet footprints.

'Oh dear. I'd b-better wipe those up before Mr Deverall g-gets here.'

I grab my towel to help her but Leonora beats me to it. 'There you go – all dry. Have you come far in the rain, Miss Batty?'

'Thank you, dear. Not t-too far – just my usual j-journey.'

Seconds later, Max bounds in carrying a large canvas bag. He's wearing black sweats and his hair is swept off his face with a red bandana.

'Hi folks. If you've eaten as much as I have over the holidays, and been half as lazy, some of you are going to find this morning tough. But, hey, Christmas is just once a year, right?'

Everyone giggles except me.

'Don't frown, Milky Bar,' whispers Spencer. 'You'll end up looking like Batty's tights.'

I glance at Miss Batty's legs and stop frowning immediately.

Max leaves the bag in the corner and nods at Miss Batty. 'Before we start, a little bird by the name of Emmeline Topping told me it's Janet's birthday today – can I call you Janet?'

Miss Batty turns scarlet.

'Janet's been here for . . . how long now?'

'Five years as a s-student, and sixteen as a p-pianist, Mr Deverall.'

Lottie stops slurping from her water bottle. 'Batty studied here?'

'Did you hear that, folks?' says Max. 'That adds up to twenty-one years of service. It deserves a song, don't you think?' He takes a breath. '*Happy Birthday to you . . .*'

My toes curl as Max begins to croon. Then Leonora joins in and everyone starts to sing. Spencer bellows over the rest:

'*Squashed tomatoes and stew,*
You'll get belly ache from Cook's birthday cake,
So stay close to the looooo.'

Poor Miss Batty squirms like she needs the loo right now.

'Do you know how old she is?' I ask Lottie.

'Hard to tell, but my Aunty Dot wears tights like that, and she's ancient,' says Lottie.

'She's only thirty-two, Lottie,' says Leonora Know-it-all. 'At least that's what Topsy told Dad this morning.'

Lottie shakes her head. 'Like I said. Ancient.'

'Thank you, everyone,' says Max. 'OK, birthday girl, let's begin.'

He takes us through our *pliés*, our *tendus* and our *glissés*. I feel the stretch through my arms, my legs and my feet. Slowly the exercises get harder and faster. I wish I could stretch away the Deveralls, but my stomach is too knotty.

Max calls us to the centre and divides us into groups of three. He watches us practise our *pirouettes* then our jumps. They start small but get bigger and bigger until we're taking it in turns to *grand jeté* across the floor. Sweat trickles down my back.

'Feel the floor, everyone! That's right! Next group!'

My turn again. I feel the air on my face, the length of my neck, the stretch in my thighs.

I smile at my reflection but then I see Leonora. She's practically flying.

'Great, Leo,' says Max. 'Milly, drop those shoulders! OK, let's leave it there. Thank you, Janet, you can go now.'

'B-but I thought we were rehearsing *The Nutcracker*, Mr D-deverall.'

'Next time, Janet, and please call me Max.'

Miss Batty gathers her sheet music and Max claps his hands. 'OK, everyone. As we're still waiting for the pleasure of the inspector's company, I'll give you an introduction to fencing. Has anyone used swords before?'

Spencer raises his hand. 'I was top of the class in my last school.'

'Name?'

'Benedict Spencer, but please call me Spencer.' Spencer does a perfect impression of Max's drawl.

Bumble snorts behind me and for the briefest moment, the bonfire in Max's eyes flares. 'In that case, *Spencer*, you can help me to demonstrate the basics.'

Spencer winks at Lottie. 'Watch and learn, Shorty – watch and learn.'

Max delves inside the canvas bag. He pulls out a couple of masks and a pair of glinting swords.

'Are they real?' I whisper.

'Of course they are,' hisses Bumble. 'A plastic sword isn't going to hurt anyone, is it?'

'This is considered the best sword for beginners,' says Max, balancing the sword lightly in his hand. 'It's called a foil.'

I jump back as he slices the air with a swish.

Max grins. 'Milly's right to be scared – fencing's a dangerous sport. So when you're not fighting, keep your weapon pointed at the ground and watch out for people around you.'

Max throws Spencer a mask and pulls one over his own face. 'Spencer, catch!'

Spencer snatches a sword from the air.

Max laughs through the mesh. 'Well done. You've passed the first test. Fencing requires lightning reflexes. Now adopt the *en garde* position.'

Spencer shifts his feet and bends his knees.

'Look, everyone, see how Spencer is standing. His sword arm is nice and loose in front of him. That's great, Spencer. I can tell you've done this before.'

Spencer grunts in his mask.

'In competition, fencing begins and ends with good manners. Before and after every bout, the fencers salute each other like this.'

Max faces Spencer. Then he holds his blade up in front of his right eye before bringing it down again.

'The aim is to score a hit, or *touché*. Your target is anywhere above your opponent's waist. There are lots of rules about how a *touché* is judged, but for now, all you need to know is that what I say goes.'

I roll my eyes.

'The three basic moves are the advance, the retreat and the lunge. When you block an incoming attack, that's called a parry. You know all this, right, Spencer?'

Spencer nods.

'Good. So, let's see your footwork. You should find this comes naturally. Of all the armed combat disciplines, fencing is the closest one to dance.'

Spencer shuffles back and forth, but suddenly Max springs forward. His blade brushes Spencer's arm, his chest, his chin. It knocks Spencer's sword out of his hands with a clatter that breaks everyone's smiles.

As Spencer falls back, Max bounds forward and points the tip of his sword at his neck.

Spencer pulls up his visor and splutters. 'You didn't say *en garde*!'

Max lifts his sword and addresses us all. 'Spencer just made the potentially fatal mistake of treating the bout like a competition. But espionage isn't a game. Fighting onstage is one thing, but when you're in the field, you'll be fighting for your lives. Never assume otherwise. Today's lesson: forget the good manners – there are no rules.'

Max leans over Spencer and pulls him up. 'No hard feelings, Spence.'

'Of course not,' says Spencer, tugging off his mask. Then to Max's amusement, he throws his mask at the wall and storms out of the door.

Lottie and I run after him, but he's gone.

By the afternoon, I'm hurting all over. Whoever said muscles have memories clearly doesn't know what they're talking about. It's only been two weeks, but mine have amnesia. I wonder if they're staying with a nice family in Piccadilly or thereabouts.

I shift in my seat at the back of the Captain's new classroom. Spencer sits stony-faced next to me.

'Is he sulkin'?' whispers Lottie.

Spencer flicks his pen at her chair.

I think he's sulking.

The Captain perches on his desk and it groans under his weight. 'This afternoon, we're going to study Cryptography,' he says. 'Can anyone tell us what that means?'

Leonora puts up her hand. 'The word is taken from the Greek *kryptos*, meaning hidden, and *graphia*, meaning writing. It's the study of enciphering and encoding, or deciphering and decoding – depending on whether you're on on the sending or receiving end.'

Smarty-pants.

'Excellent,' says the Captain. 'Could you give us some examples?'

As Leonora shows off her IQ, I think back to the floor pattern in *The Secrets of Swan House*. The title was in code, *NSKA BLCN BSRE*. I scribble it down on my notepad – if I concentrate I might learn how to decipher it? But so far, I haven't understood a single word Leonora has said. I start doodling instead.

'Kydd, are you with us?' says the Captain.

I'm saved from answering by an angry red flash on his Swanphone.

Something is wrong.

Very.

12

The House Fell Down

The Captain grabs his bag. 'Pack up, class, and follow us.'

Nervous laughter spills into the corridors. I'm swept along with the tide of bodies on the stairs.

The Captain holds open the door of Ms Celia's studio.

I spot Max and Ms Celia whispering next to the piano.

'Move all the way to the back, we've got to squeeze everyone in,' orders the Captain.

Spencer and I get shuffled behind Ms Celia and I catch her say, 'And you're sure no one followed you yesterday?'

'Positive,' replies Max. 'I went straight to Meekes, got everything I needed for Leonora from Dorothy, then came straight back.'

Came straight back? Did Max Deverall just tell

Ms Celia a big, fat lie? I score him an eleven out of ten on the fib-o-meter.

Ms Celia holds up her hand. 'Quiet, everyone, please. This morning, I received a communication. You are here because while the meaning is unclear, the urgency is not. I need every single one of you to work on its decryption. Please gather around.'

Decryption? I may as well leave right now.

All eyes are on Ms Celia as she rolls up the sleeve of her shirt and points her Swanphone towards the piano.

A large, leather-bound book appears on the piano stool. It's the colour of midnight and embossed in gold.

Everyone *ahhh*s. It's not just a hologram.

It's *The Guide to Espionage*.

Ms Celia watches the virtual pages turn one by one. 'For those of you at the back, the book is about to fall open on pages seven and eight. Rule Four.'

'Rule Four? That's *Think outside the box*,' says Spencer.

'That's correct, but the text underneath Rule Four has been replaced with something more cryptic. Max, would you care to read out the page to the students?'

Max clears his throat.

'*Rule Four. Think outside the box:*

Hickory Dickory Dock,
The mouse ran up the clock,
The clock struck one,
The house fell down,
Hickory Dickory Dock.'

I jump as the book slams shut.

Spencer laughs. 'It's just a nursery rhyme.'

Max's eyes blaze in Spencer's direction. 'You think this is funny, Spencer? Believe me, it's no laughing matter. The hologram was sent by a villain who goes by the name of the Mouse King. Most of you won't have heard of him, but for years he played a cat-and-mouse game with Swan House. He specialized in disinformation, fake news. He pitted one state against another, leaving a trail of chaos and destruction behind him. Then eleven years ago, he disappeared.' Max clicks his fingers. 'Just like that.'

'Until Christmas, that is,' adds Ms Celia with a look that shrinks Spencer by at least ten centimetres. 'Some of you may have spotted that the fourth line of the riddle differs from the nursery rhyme.'

Leonora puts up her hand. I don't know why she doesn't just keep it there.

'In the original, the line was "the mouse ran down", not "the house fell down". It sounds like the Mouse King plans to destroy some kind of building.'

Ms Celia nods. 'My thoughts exactly, Leonora. He

may have hidden more fireworks in a repeat of the incident at the Royal Opera House. But I suspect that his next attack will be far more deadly. The question we must focus on is, *where?* Where is this building? Something in the riddle will tell us where to look.' She checks her Swanphone. 'It is now 1500 hours. It would seem that we have until the clock next strikes one to find it. I want the whole school on the job.'

She rolls down her sleeve and the book disappears. 'You'll find all the resources you you need in the sixth form common room. Captain, Max, please escort the children there post-haste.'

The sixth-form common room? Isn't that where Tom Garrick visited the virtual library?

Leonora dashes into the corridor with Max. The rest of us hurry after the Captain.

Lottie finds me at the bottom of the stairs. 'What do you fink this Mouse King's up to?'

'I don't know, but Mum's trying to find out. I wasn't allowed to tell you before, but the reason she went away over Christmas is because Max had a hunch about where he is.'

Lottie pauses. 'Sorry, Milly, I never realized.'

'Hey, you two!' Spencer runs up behind us. His voice is still smarting from Max's telling off. 'Either of you know why we've got to go to the common room? A bunch of bean bags and a couple of dart boards aren't going to solve the riddle, are they?'

'Actually, Spence, the only things in the common room are books.'

'How would you know?' says Spencer.

I wait until everyone has pushed ahead and tell Lottie and Spencer about Tom Garrick and the compact drone.

'What d'you mean it's a key?' says Lottie.

Spencer perks up. 'Are you saying that whoever has the drone has clearance to go *anywhere*?'

'Yep.'

'Can I borrow it?'

'No.'

'Please.'

'Not unless you need it for something important.'

Spencer grins. 'I'll think of something. Like bringing down Max Deverall a peg or two for a start.'

'What do you want to do that for?' says Lottie.

'Because he doesn't play fair.'

'And he's a liar,' I say, thinking about Max's disappearing act yesterday.

Lottie frowns. 'What are you on about?'

'KYDD, LI, SPENCER! HERE – NOW!' The Captain's voice booms down the corridor.

'I'll tell you later.'

13

The Virtual Library

The common room is hot and stuffy and smells of eggs – probably because it's directly above the refectory. It's all threadbare carpet, old wooden tables, shabby chairs and saggy sofas. Not a bean bag or dartboard in sight.

'Watch this,' I say to Lottie and Spencer as the Captain shouts over our heads.

'OPEN THE VIRTUAL LIBRARY!'

Lottie groans. 'I *hate* flamin' libraries.'

'I'm with her,' says Spencer.

I sweep my hand along the glowing shelves that the Captain seems to have conjured out of thin air. 'But this is amazing.'

'Sit down, everyone,' says Max. 'It's already 1500 hours. That's less than ten hours to crack the code. Let's get to work.'

I grab a table and push back a chair for Lottie.

'Fanks,' says Lottie. 'Over here, Leonora!'

I heave a sigh. I'll never be able to talk to Lottie about Max at this rate.

Merv follows Leonora and Spencer follows Merv. 'If we're going to be cracking codes, I want to be with the two geniuses in the room,' he says.

Something tells me he's not talking about Lottie and me.

Leonora's eyes travel from the floor to the ceiling and rest on the shimmering bookcases in between. 'It's *beautiful*.'

Merv's monobrow sighs.

The virtual librarian appears at the top of a ladder. There's a gasp as she whooshes towards the Captain.

'Who said they dinnae like libraries? Where can ye travel from Glesga to Bangkok in less than five minutes? Or get inside the heid of an actual *genius*?' She pushes her little round glasses up her virtual nose. 'Libraries should blow yer wee minds! And this is the library to end all libraries – there's stuff in Swan Hoose that's been classified for more than three hunner years!'

'Obviously, access to classified material has to be passed by us,' adds the Captain hastily. 'But you can borrow most books using your Swanphone, and if you need help, Sid knows her stuff. How long have you been in the library now, Sid?'

'Since seventy-six,' says Sid. 'Year of the Pistols.'

'Year of the what?' asks Leonora.

'Go look them up. Music section, under P for Punk.'

'Sid, make sure everyone has a copy of the riddle,' says the Captain.

Sid's Mohican brushes the spines of the books as she cocks her head. 'Ye'll have to ask me nicer than that, Garth Thurgood – and keep yer voice doon, big man – we're in a library, remember?'

'*Please*, Sid,' whispers the Captain meekly.

'Listen to him. She's got the "big man" wrapped around her little finger,' says Spencer.

Lottie nods thoughtfully. 'Maybe libraries ain't so bad after all.'

The ladder slides to the opposite wall. Sid gathers copies of the Mouse King's version of *The Guide to Espionage* and starts to hand them out.

On another table, I hear Jada Gayle tell her copy to open at page seven. I do the same and seconds later, I'm staring at the Mouse King's riddle.

RULE 4.
Think outside the box

Hickory dickory dock,
The mouse ran up the clock,
The clock struck one,
The house fell down,
Hickory dickory dock.

Fig 15.

7

8

Merv mutters at his Swanphone and unpadlocks his satchel. He pulls out a battered old laptop and starts typing at a Mervillion miles an hour.

The Captain paces between the tables. 'Merv's not the only one with a brain around here. Switch on your mentors, everyone. Some of them became world-class codebreakers.'

Seconds later there are twice as many people in the library. The virtual ones mull around the bookshelves and peer over shoulders.

Leonora follows Dafydd to the nearest bookcase. Ivan Korolev takes a seat next to Spencer. A lock of blue-bottle black hair falls over his eyes. 'Ve vill solve the riddle first. I know everything there is to know about *The Guide to Espionage*.'

'That's what you fink,' says Lottie. 'Leonora and her mum are helpin' us. You don't stand a chance.'

'Her mum?' says Spencer.

'Yeah, Nora's Leonora's mum – can you flippin' believe it?'

'But I thought Nora Doone died.'

'Keep it down, Spence. She did, but that was after she and Max'd left school and got hitched. Nora was killed just after Leonora was born.'

'What happened to her?'

'Dunno,' says Lottie, 'it's classified.'

The Captain growls at me from across the table.

'Where's your mentor, Kydd? We need all hands on deck. Yours too, Crump.'

I haven't seen Merv's mentor for ages. Partly because Merv's so clever he doesn't need one. But mostly because Han Wu scares the Crump out of him.

Merv yelps as Han Wu bows through his laptop. 'Wish the MNTR program would give *me* a new mentor.'

I switch on Trevor and sigh. I know how he feels.

'Greetings, Milly! How can I help you?'

Ivan scowls. 'Is that *Topping* – the vorld-class *loser*?'

Everyone looks up from their books. Bumble laughs out loud.

Trevor's beam doesn't dip an inch. 'Never judge a book by its cover, Ivan.'

'Thanks for the advice, my friend, but I don't need you to tell me vhat's in *The Guide to Espionage*.'

Trevor peers at the book. 'It's a poem, isn't it? I like a bit of poetry, me.' He clears his throat. '*I wandered lonely as a cloud . . .*'

I sigh and wish he had something between *his* covers. 'It's not that kind of poem, Trevor. It's a nursery rhyme.'

'Is it? Between you and me, I'm more of a numbers man.'

'Listen, it doesn't matter. It's probably another

silly hoax. I'm never going to solve it anyway.'

'Now don't say that, Milly. Try, try, try again, that's what we Toppings say.'

I do try and try again but a couple of hours later I still haven't got anywhere. Across the table, Merv puts his laptop back in his satchel and pushes back his chair.

'Where are you going?' asks Spencer.

'Back to the CR. It's been a very long day.'

'The where?' asks Leonora.

Spencer explains. 'The control room overlooking the theatre. It's where all the computers and surveillance stuff is. It's Merv's happy place.'

The Captain looms over Merv. 'Solved it already, have you, son?'

Merv's monobrow arches like a very intelligent caterpillar. 'In all likelihood, the riddle is encrypted. I've fed the data into my Swanphone and linked it to the hard drives at the CIA, MSS and GCHQ. You'll have your answer by bedtime.'

He lopes across the library and disappears into the corridor with the Captain calling after him. 'Your digital jiggery-pokery'd better work, Crump. Come back as soon as you have the answer!'

Supper time comes and goes. Cook and Topsy arrive with watery hot chocolate and plates of raisin cookies that taste like squashed flies. The day's gone and I have nothing to show for it except pins and needles in my feet and pages of doodles of fat, ginger cats. My mind isn't just wandering – it's off on a ten-mile trek. It's at times like these it would be nice to have a mentor with half a brain – put our heads together and we might actually have a whole one. To make matters worse, Trevor keeps popping on and off in the most discombobulating way. I know he was an early prototype, but this is a joke.

Lottie and Nora are cosied up at the other end of the table with Leonora and Dafydd. They haven't stopped making notes since we got here.

Why oh why did Nora have to be Leonora's mum? A not very nice part of me hopes Merv's digital jiggery-pokery solves the riddle before she does.

Suddenly Max leaps up. 'Captain, I've just had a thought. There's a big old clock in my study – isn't it possible that the "house" in the riddle is Swan House?'

'Unlikely,' replies the Captain, 'but you'd better check it out.'

Unlikely? More like impossible. Even the Mouse King isn't clever enough to plant a bomb in Swan House. I yawn loudly. The words *hickory dickory dock* are seared on to my eyeballs. Keeping my eyelids open is virtually impossi . . . The Captain bangs the table. 'Kydd, I wouldn't nod off unless you want to end up on the Dance of Death tonight. I'm told that concentrates the mind.'

I bolt up and try my hardest not to blink. The last student to *jeté* along the scary barbed wire fence that runs around the school boundary left the obstacle course in an ambulance and didn't come back.

The Captain flips through my notepad and makes the sort of noise that rattles your insides. It's like rush hour on the Northern Line.

'Don't think you can slack off just because you were the glory girl last term. Time is ticking!'

'Sorry, Captain. I am trying, but codes aren't really my thing.'

'Aren't your *thing*?' My stomach rattles again. 'Then what's that?'

He prods my pad with a great, gnarly finger.

Uh-oh. It's the title of the floor pattern – *NSKA BLCN BSRE.*

'If you can use the Swancode to *en*code, you can bliddy well use your little grey cells to *de*code.'

Encode? Decode? The Swancode? What's he talking about? I need to find Merv, he'd know.

I nod enthusiastically. 'Will do, Captain, but can I please be excused to go to the loo first?'

The Captain shakes his head. 'Get out of here.'

'She can use ours, they're closer,' says Jada Gayle.

I give her a grateful smile. The sixth-form loos are on the way up to the CR.

Trevor starts to follow me. 'Like I said Milly, I'm a numbers man and—'

'I know, Trevor, you already said.'

Leonora looks up from her pad. 'What did you just say, Trevor?'

'Ah, greetings, Leonora. I was just saying to Milly that I'm a numbers man and if you look at pages—'

'We *know*, Trevor. Pages seven and eight.' I switch him off. 'Sorry, Leonora – got to go!'

I make my way to the staircase, but I don't get further than the loos. Huddled around the corner is Max Deverall. He's whispering into a phone that isn't a Swanphone. It's not even a smartphone. It's an old dumbphone like the Bombardier's.

I flatten myself against the wall like a proper spy.

'I looked for you in the Royal Opera House but you'd gone,' he says. 'Meet me on Wednesday, 1300 hours. Make sure you're not seen. OK. Got to get back.'

Max puts the phone in his pocket and I slip into the girl's loo.

Make sure you're not seen.

First he lies to Ms Celia and now he's arranging a

secret rendezvous. This is deeply suspicious.

Mr Stubbs's words go around in my head. *Max and Korolev, thick as tea leaves, terrors they was.* Was that before or after Korolev changed sides? What in Swan House is Max Deverall up to?

14

Thinking Outside the Box

Wait until Lottie hears about this. I knew the Deveralls were too good to be true!

I run back to the library, surprised by how relieved the Captain is to see me. Then I realize he's not looking at me. Merv is right behind me.

'Did you decypher it, son?'

Merv shakes his head.

'Have you got anything at all?'

Merv rubs his eyes.

'Talk, man!'

'I haven't got anything. The program didn't work.'

'THEN SIT DOWN AND WRITE A NEW ONE! PEOPLE'S LIVES COULD BE AT STAKE!'

'STOP SHOUTING!' shouts Merv. 'I don't work well under pressure.'

The Captain wipes his forehead and Merv slumps next to Spencer. I hover over Lottie. Sheets of paper are strewn all over the table. Pages and pages of scribbled little symbols in Leonora's handwriting.

'Where've you been, Milky Bar?' asks Spencer.

'The loo.'

Lottie frowns. 'You were ages.'

'That's because I saw something.' I glance at Supergirl. 'Lottie, come with me, I've got something to tell you.'

'Just a minute.' Leonora grabs Lottie's arm and points at her copy of the book. 'This is beginning to make sense. Look at the box.'

I grab Lottie's other arm. 'This can't wait.'

Lottie shakes me off. 'You should be tryin' to solve the riddle like rest of us,' she says. 'Tell me what you saw later.'

The Captain cracks his knuckles behind me. 'Head down, Kydd. Don't forget what I said about the Dance of Death.'

I flump in my chair and scribble so hard my pen goes through the paper.

Wednesday, one o'clock. Max suspicious rendezvous with ???

I'll show Lottie what the Deveralls are really like.

The countdown on our Swanphones flashes by. Every now and then, Merv moans to himself.

'Are you OK, Merv?' I ask.

Merv moans again. 'My emotional state must be interfering with my powers of logic. I can't think outside the box – I can't think *inside* the box!'

I nod in sympathy. Let's face it, if GCHQ, the CIA, the MSS (whoever they are) and our Swanphones can't solve the riddle, what chance have I got?

The Captain continues to pace but his legs are so long he keeps walking through virtual bookcases. 'Come on, everyone, it's almost midnight! We've got less than an hour to reach the location and disarm the device! What is it, Bee?'

Bumble is waggling her arm in the air. 'I'VE CRACKED THE RIDDLE. It's in the Houses of Parliament. There's a bomb in Big Ben!'

Leonora stands up. 'No, it's not.' She grabs her hoody and glances at me. 'I know where it is. I've found the location.'

'Where?' says Max, ignoring Bumble's grumbling.

Somehow I already know what Leonora's going to say.

'Sorry, Milly. It's in your house.'

'Well, that's the most stupid idea I ever heard,' says Bumble.

I knock back my chair. *Bab!* 'Bab's at home all alone.'

Everyone starts talking at once.

'QUIET!' booms the Captain.

Max is already on his phone. A ringtone fills the silence. I know who he's calling and my whole body tenses.

Bab, please, PLEASE pick up the phone.

'No answer,' says Max. 'She must be asleep.'

'Are you sure about this, Leonora?' says the Captain.

'Of course she is,' says Max, backing out. 'She knows what she's doing. Let's go!'

The Captain nods and calls Ms Celia. Then they all dash into the corridor with me chasing after them on legs that feel like they belong to somebody else.

We all pour into the night. It's inky black. No moon. No stars. Not the tiniest beam of light.

An engine rumbles, then a bright white light illuminates the courtyard. I blink. The headlights belong to Winifred but the machine in front of me doesn't look like Winifred. Since Monday afternoon, she's acquired wings and a tail. Like one of those fighter jets you see in air displays.

Bab would LOVE to be rescued by one of those.

The Captain squashes into the front. The Deveralls jump into the back. Ms Celia opens the driver's door, or pilot's door – or whatever it is.

Still running, I yell out, 'Ms Celia, wait! You've got to take me with you!'

'I'm sorry, Milly, this job calls for our best agents.'

'But Bab's my grandmother. She needs me!'

Max's window slides open. 'Bab needs someone who can diffuse a bomb and deploy the weapons on their Swanphone. She needs someone who can think on their feet.'

I might not know how to diffuse a bomb or use the weapons on my Swanphone, but I can think on my feet. I've done it before.

Ms Celia's door slams shut and Winifred starts to roar. There's a blast of wind and she lifts into the air – up and up, hovering over me and my sticky-up hair like a helicopter. Then with an ear-bending *BOOM* she's gone.

Wait a minute – a helicopter? I've got one of those!

I race into the dorm. It's here. In my trunk. I was going to give it back to Merv, but it might still work. It *has* to work! I fling out my clothes and find it right at the bottom.

The door bursts open. Lottie looks from me to the scraps of metal and silk in my hands. 'Milly, what are you doin'?'

'Lottie, help me put this on, would you? It's the only way I can get home!'

Lottie looks doubtful. 'What is it?'

I shake it out. The skirt is in tatters but the hoops and blades are still in one piece.

'It's the flying tutu Merv stole from Madge last term. It got me home once. I'm sure it can do it again.'

'It don't look safe to dance in, let alone fly in.'

'It's the only way. Please, Lottie!'

Moments later, we're in the courtyard. I press the ignition button over my breastbone and the tutu quivers. But as I brace myself to be lifted into the air, it stalls.

'I don't like it, Milly,' says Lottie. 'Sounds worse than my mum's old Rover and she's got to jump start that every mornin'.'

'Jump start . . . genius idea!' I press the ignition again and jump up and down. As the blades start to whirr, my body vibrates.

'Fink you need annuver plan!' shouts Lottie over the squeaks, but I'm not listening. I don't want to listen. I'm too scared for Bab and Boris to be scared for me.

Lottie gawps as I fly over her head. Up and up, until she's a tiny dot. I skim over the roof, away from the lights in the common room and into the big black sky.

I imagine Bab all tucked up in bed and Boris at her feet. 'HURRY UP!' I yell at my tutu.

It answers with a cough.

Uh-oh. I notice the wispy vapour trail of netting behind me.

It coughs again and I drop a metre.

It coughs some more then stops.

This is bad.

Very.

I start to plummet. The air roars in my ears. Down and down I spin. Closer and closer to the lake.

My mouth screams a scream no one can hear. '*Garghhh!* Not again!'

Suddenly, the tutu jerks to a stop and I dangle like a puppet on invisible strings. Then the strings break, and I fall feet first into the icy, black water.

I hold my breath as my toes hit the bottom. The weeds catch my tutu and I tug at the net. Lungs burning, I pull one last time and spiral towards the surface.

'Milly!' shouts a voice in the dark. 'Milly, this way!'

Light zig-zags across the lake. Gulping for air, I take a few desperate strokes until my feet find the bottom.

As I wade towards the light, two dark figures run towards me.

Lottie splashes into the shallows and holds out her hand. 'You OK?'

My bones ache with cold and I keep sliding backwards down the bank.

'F-fine,' I say, shivering all over. 'But I've got to get home to B-Bab.'

Spencer takes my other arm. 'Sorry, Kydd. It's too late. It's gone one o'clock. We should hear back from Ms Celia any second.'

Lottie puts an arm around my waist. 'Don't worry – she won't let nuffink happen to her.'

Don't worry? I try to smile through chattering teeth.

There's a shout from the woods and a startled moon-white swan beats its wings in warning. Merv staggers through the trees. 'Kydd! Got a message from the Captain.' He stops to pant. 'Your grandmother –' he pants some more – 'she's fine.'

I sit down right where I am and let out a sob.

Merv starts to hum.

'Go on, we'll catch you up,' says Lottie to the boys. She wraps her hoody around me and we sit there without saying a word until I'm ready to get up again.

'How did you know where to find me?' I ask as we trek back through the mud.

'Merv was trackin' your Swanphone. When he saw you comin' down, we legged it into the woods.' She grins at my tutu. 'It's goin' to take more than a couple of Sid's safety pins to fix that. An' have you seen your knees? You'd better see Nurse.'

It's not just my knees that are criss-crossed in scratches. The backs of my hands are bleeding too and there's blood on my Swanphone. I wonder if that's why it's flashing, but it's a message from Ms Celia:

Your grandmother is alive and none the wiser.
Will debrief first thing a.m. Go to bed!

I wait impatiently for Nurse to clean up my cuts. I want to talk to Lottie about Max, but before I get the chance, Supergirl is back in the dorm and can't wait to tell us what happened.

'What did Bab say? Was she all right?' I tuck my blankets under my chin and fan my damp bob on the pillow.

Leonora puts her shoes neatly at the end of her bed. 'Bab didn't even wake up. It was so sweet – Boris was outside her bedroom door, like a guard cat.'

I hug my hot-water Boris and whisper a well done.

'And where was the bomb?' asks Lottie.

'Inside the hall clock. But it wasn't a bomb.'

'Wait a minute,' says Lottie. 'Did you say it *wasn't* a bomb?'

'Not even close. It was just a doll.'

Lottie and I both frown. 'A doll?'

'A little Nutcracker doll – like in the ballet.'

'Why would the Mouse King leave a doll?' I say.

'I don't know, Milly. It seemed pretty harmless to me, but it was weird – Ms Celia looked really worried. Dad gave it to Madge to examine. I guess the Mouse King was just playing games with us again.'

'Then I wish he'd play with some other family.' I shoot her an accusing look. 'Especially while Mum's not here.'

'Go easy, Milly. Leonora's the one who worked out Bab was in danger.'

'It's OK,' says Leonora. 'I was worried about Bab too, but Eva just spoke to Dad. She said she'd reached a dead end so she should be back soon.'

'She spoke to Max?'

'Yes, for ages.'

Grrr.

'That's good, ain't it, Milly? says Lottie with a yawn. 'But just one more fing before I conk out – Leo, how did you figure out the riddle?'

Leonora orders her Swanphone to show us a snapshot of the book. 'Rule Four is *think outside the box*, right? Look, there's a gold keyline around the riddle. With a little help, I realized it was all about the numbers outside of that box. See. *Four. Seven. Eight.*

And *fifteen*. Turns out the fourth, seventh, eighth and fifteenth letters of the riddle are K, Y, D, D. Obvious, really.'

I roll my eyes. I bet her mentor was loads of help. 'You're so lucky to have Dafydd.'

'Oh, it wasn't Dafydd who gave me the idea,' says Leonora meekly. 'It was Trevor.'

'Trevor?'

'You're jokin', ain't you?' says Lottie.

'He said he was a numbers man, remember? So I started focusing on the numbers on the page, rather than the letters. I know you were disappointed to get Trevor's avatar, Milly, but Dad said Mum worked with him a lot. Apparently she had a real soft spot for him, so he couldn't have been *that* bad.'

'She probably felt sorry for him,' I say. But what I'm thinking is, *Leonora wouldn't have needed any help to solve the riddle IF SHE ALREADY KNEW THE ANSWER.*

My brain starts to tick louder than a grandfather clock. Who was at the Royal Opera House when the Mouse King's fireworks went off? Who had oodles of opportunity to plant something in my house? Who is behaving in a deeply suspicious manner?

Max and Leonora Deverall, that's who.

Is it possible – just possible, they could be working with the Mouse King?

Or is it possible – just possible, that Max could *be* the Mouse King?

Lottie turns off the light. 'We need a list of suspects. There can't be many people who know you and your mum are spies, Milly.'

I nod in the dark. If I was a numbers man, I'd narrow the suspects down to two.

15

The School Inspector

The next day starts with brilliant news and bad news.

The brilliant news is that Mum sent me a message:

So relieved you and Bab are safe. All is well here, please try not to worry about me. I'll be out of reach for a little while, but hope to be home soon. Love, Mum xx

OK, so she didn't say where 'here' was, but at least she got in touch. The bad news is that she messaged Leonora too.

Leonora reads it out loud on our way to breakfast.

Well done for solving the riddle. Wish I could thank you in person. Much love, Eva xx

Much love. Kiss, kiss . . . Huh. Mum wouldn't have written that if she knew what I know.

When we reach the refectory, Supergirl is practically mobbed over the breakfast counter.

'Come and sit with us,' says Fleur. 'I could do with some intelligent conversation.'

Bumble grumbles behind her. 'Fleur Fontaine, are you calling me stupid?'

'Yes. I mean, no. I mean come with us, Leonora . . .' Poor Fleur. She's getting herself into a muddle because Bumble is jabbing her arm with a fork.

'Go on, Leonora,' I say. 'You've only been here a couple of days and it's good to make lots of friends, isn't it – when you're new?'

'What's she want to make friends wiv Bumble for?' says Lottie. 'Spencer's saved us a table, sit wiv us, Leonora.'

Leonora takes one look at the little prong marks on Fleur's arm and comes with us.

I stare at my breakfast. According to Cook, kedgeree is 'a delicious mix of curried rice, smoked fish and boiled eggs brought over from India in Victorian times'.

Looks like cat sick to me.

'Sorry about the nosh,' says Lottie, 'Cook can't cook for toffee.'

'I'd kill for toffee right now,' says Spencer. 'You got any of those Russian biscuits left, Milky Bar?'

Leonora puts a whole spoonful of cat sick in her mouth. 'It's not so bad. When Dad and I were in the Gobi Desert, we ate nothing but scorpions for weeks.'

'You ate *scorpions*?' says Lottie. She thumps Leonora's arm and my insides go cold.

What's so cool about eating scorpions? Why couldn't they have taken cheese sandwiches like normal people? A little voice inside my head says, *Because they're not normal people, that's why.* I glance at the time. Only five hours until midday and I still haven't had a chance to tell Lottie about Max's secret rendezvous.

Lottie burps her way through her cat sick. I stick to my toast, scraping off the burnt bits while Leonora tells us stories. She's like Leonora Jones and the Temple of Doom. Suddenly, she stops mid-sentence.

'Go on. What happened after you escaped from the volcano?' asks Lottie.

'Sorry, Lottie, did anyone notice how everyone's mentors just switched off?'

Our Swanphones flash all at once.

'The inspector's here!' I say happily. As far as I'm concerned this is a win-win situation. It shuts up Leonora and means no more Trevor Topping for the foreseeable future.

Spencer nods at the door. 'Speak of the devil . . .'

I turn to see a man with horn-rimmed glasses and

a thin, brown moustache creep towards the counter. His thin brown hair is combed to one side. His gravy-brown suit is neatly pressed.

He lifts a lid from one of the silver domes.

He sniffs and wrinkles his nose.

He writes something on his clipboard.

The refectory doors bang and Topsy comes charging in. Apart from her bright pink nose, her face is white and shiny.

'Oh, there you are, Bister Brown,' she wheezes. 'I thought I'd lost you! Cub with be, please-thank-you.'

'I prefer to be left to my own devices, thank you, Miss Topping,' says the man in a cotton-wool voice.

Topsy's eyes shoot up to the ceiling. 'But Bizz Celia said you should stay with be at ALL TIBES . . . it's dangerous you see—'

'She's talking about the lasers,' says Spencer to Leonora.

'SHHH,' says Lottie. 'I'm tryin' to listen.'

'Dangerous?' says Mr Brown.

'Well, not *dangerous* exactly.'

'Don't worry, Miss Topping, I have my own methods of dealing with unruly children.'

We swap looks. Unruly children?

'Oh dear.' Topsy sits down. 'Is it hot in here? I'b ever so hot.'

'Unlike the food,' says Mr Brown inspecting a

piece of cremated toast. He tuts. 'I don't think I will have breakfast after all. The quality of school meals is so often in line with the quality of its education, don't you agree, Miss Topping?'

Topsy fans herself with a napkin. 'Oh yes! That's why Bubby – I bean Cook– taught herself to bake everythig frob scratch.'

'No for-mal train-ing,' says Mr Brown, scribbling on his clipboard. He checks his watch. 'I have twenty unscheduled minutes before classes begin so I suppose you could escort me to some alternative accommodation.'

'But Bizz Celia gave you Lord Astus's suite – it's the best in the school . . .'

Mr Brown rocks on his heels. 'Lord Astus may have enjoyed sharing a room with a suit of rusty armour and an array of dusty weaponry, but I favour *modern*, *hygienic* conveniences, Miss Topping.'

'Oh dear,' says Topsy again. 'We'd better find Bizz Celia.'

Mr Brown slips his biro into his jacket pocket. 'I think we better had.'

'What a sneak,' whispers Lottie, as Mr Brown scuttles past.

Leonora sucks on her spoon. 'He reminds me of someone . . .'

I check my Swanphone again. I'm running out of

time. 'Lottie, want to come back to the dorm? I've *uhh* – forgotten something.'

'What did you forget?' asks Lottie.

'Come with me and I'll show you.'

She whispers in my ear. 'What is it, Milly? You've been actin' real odd since the Deveralls got here. It ain't like you.'

I whisper back. 'If you weren't with Leonora every second, I could explain.'

Lottie's dimples vanish. 'What's that s'posed to mean?'

'I remember!' Leonora exclaims. 'Mr Brown looks exactly like a triple agent who betrayed us in Prague once. Did I tell you that story, Lottie?'

'A triple agent?' Lottie shuffles her chair closer to Leonora's.

Grrr. Looks like I'm on my own. But how am I going to trail Max without being seen? I gaze down at my plate and an idea pops into my head like a burnt piece of toast.

If Lottie won't help me, I know someone who will.

Outside the control room, I say a little prayer to my geek god.

'Dear Merv, who art from Devon, please don't

132

let me down.'

Inside, Merv's got his nose in a virtual book. Behind him, rows of computer screens snooze in the shadows. Down in the theatre, the inspector follows Ms Celia through the side door that leads to Lord Astus's suite.

'Do you know who they remind me of?' I nod at the dreaming monitors. 'Leonora. She sleeps with one eye open too.'

'No she doesn't,' Merv grunts. 'Unless you're trying to be metaphorical, in which case, she probably does.'

As usual, I have no idea what he's talking about. 'What are you reading?'

'*The Tools of the Trade*. It was written by the old Shoe Keeper.'

'Ooo. Is that Hugo Kinsmeet? I don't suppose there's anything in there about avatars? Trevor's definitely broken.'

'I'll take a look,' sighs Merv.

'Thanks.' I perch on the edge of the console.

Merv squeaks. 'I've told you before, don't touch anything!'

I notice his monobrow is not it's usual wriggly self. 'Merv, are you OK?'

'If you must know, I'm at a very low ebb.'

Merv scratches his ear. 'I must be coming down

with something. Yesterday I should have made the connection between the numbers and the riddle and I didn't. That's NEVER happened to me before.'

'Have you got a sore throat?'

'No.'

'A headache?'

'No, but I've got an itch behind my left year. And now I can't work out the Nutcracker doll either. It's got to be a puzzle, but Madge and I can't unlock it.'

'Merv, I'm sure you'll work it out soon. Can we talk about something else? I need a teeny-tiny favour.'

'Oh, it's all you, you, you,' sniffs Merv. 'What kind of teeny-tiny favour?'

'You must promise not to tell. It's very hush hush, etcetera etcetera.'

Merv folds his arms. 'Is it important?'

I fold my arms too. 'Very important, extremely important, nationally important, er probably. Look, Merv, I need to borrow your Universal Magnetic Blocker.'

I'm not sure if the moaning noise is Merv, or if his monitor is overheating.

'Why?'

'I have to follow someone. If I have MUMB, I'll be able to get around the school without anyone knowing, won't I? I promise you'll have it back by teatime.'

Merv stops moaning and has a little argument with himself. I cross my fingers behind my back and hope he doesn't ask who I want to follow.

'... *No, yes, no, yes, noooo-kaaaay.* But you have to look after it. And follow my exact instructions. And not get caught. Can you do that?'

'Yes?'

'Do you promise?'

'I promise.'

'Who do you have to follow?'

Drat.

'Like I said, it's totally top secret.'

Merv's monobrow twitches. 'Is this about Max Deverall?'

'No.'

'You're lying.'

Sigh. 'OK, yes. How did you know?'

'I saw you watching him outside the sixth-form loos.'

'You did? And didn't you find his behaviour deeply suspicious?'

'No. What's suspicious about talking on the phone?'

'But he wasn't using his Swanphone, don't you think that's weird?'

'I admit that is unusual, but I'm sure there's a very good reason.'

'Merv, he was planning a secret rendezvous. If you'll just let me have MUMB, I can prove he and Leonora are up to something.'

Merv drops his virtual book. 'Up to something? Leonora? NO WAY. The Deveralls are HEROES!'

'BUT MERV—'

'Sorry, Kydd. You're on your own.'

What is it about the Deveralls? It's like they're sprinkled with fairy dust. Oh well, I'll just have wear my beret and a pair of dark glasses.

When I get to the studio, everyone is laughing at some joke of Max's. Well, everyone except Spencer. He's probably still sore at Max for embarrassing him yesterday.

All through the warm-up, all I can think about is where Max is going, who he's meeting, what he's up to? If Madame was here, she'd be yelling at me for not concentrating, but either Max doesn't notice, or he doesn't care.

He gives us a five-minute break and Lottie sidles next to me. 'You goin' to tell me what's goin' on now?'

I open my mouth to answer but Max catches my eye. 'I can't. Not here. I'll tell you later, I promise.'

Lottie shrugs. 'Suit yourself.'

Max claps his hands. 'OK, kids, let's split into groups of girls and boys. There's a lot to get through and I want to cast the solos as quickly as possible. First of all, the Sugar Plum Fairy. She may only dance for a short time, but her solo is one of the most demanding. You'll need technique, stamina and something a little less easy to pin down . . . let's call it magic. We'll start with three of you at a time – Leonora, Milly and Amy, you first.'

As Max shows us the steps, I forget to hate him. His arms are soft. His legs are strong. He's the perfect mix of grace and power. '. . . Then *relevé*,' he says, 'keeping your *battements battu* in time with the music . . .'

I copy his movements, lightly beating my foot before lowering it back down.

'Leo, really bend your body into the *tendu*. OK, girls, let's try it from the beginning. Janet, could you play a first few bars of introduction.'

'"Dance of the Sugar Plum Fairy"?' says Miss Batty.

'That's right.'

As music tinkles from the piano, one of the sheets flutters to my feet.

I pass it back. Poor Miss Batty; her hands are freezing. She could really do with a decent coat and a pair of gloves.

Max glances at his Swanphone. 'Now remember, girls, the Sugar Plum isn't just the Queen of the Kingdom of Sweets – she's the Queen of Christmas. Use your *ports de bras* to show how regal she is. Are you ready now, Janet?'

As Miss Batty nods, I feel a hiss in my ear.

'This part is *mine*, do you hear me, Milly?'

I hiss back. 'It's Leonora you should be worried about, Bumble.'

But deep down, I want the part too. Who wouldn't want to be the Queen of Christmas?

I try to push Max's rendezvous out of my mind, but it's no good. Not that it seems to matter. All his comments are directed at Leonora. 'Leo, keep your feet sharp but soften the arms – that's right, *aaaaaand* finish.'

Leonora's finish is as crisp as a *kozulya*. Bumble and I both hrumph.

Max glances at his Swanphone and so do I.

Twelve thirty.

He picks up his jacket from a chair and slings it over his shoulder. He slaps Spencer on the back on his way out. 'You can stop sulking, Spencer. No room on my team for bad sports.'

Spencer's hands ball into angry fists.

'Well done, folks. See you tomorrow. Oh, and don't forget we've got company. Until the inspector leaves, Spy Craft will be on hold until further notice. Next lesson with the Captain is Geography.'

Everyone groans, but Max is already halfway down the corridor. Bumble makes sure to step on Leonora's toes as she leaves.

I pick up my backpack and rush into the corridor. Lottie calls after me but I don't look back. Which way did he go? I spot him as he passes Dame Anna's statue and lets himself into his study.

I hide behind the statue and wait for him to come out, but then I remember the tunnels. Mum said Max has clearance 'at the highest level' – he's bound to know about the maze of tunnels running under the school. And one of them is hidden behind the grandfather clock in his study. I have to get into his room!

The door's locked but that doesn't matter. I fumble in my bag for my compact drone – round and smooth and ready to open the door.

Glancing up at the security camera, I mouth a *sorry* at Merv and slip inside.

16

The Secret Rendezvous

As I suspected, our new Head of Ballet is nowhere to be been.

If Merv was right and Max was making an innocent phone call, why would he be sneaking about in the tunnels? Why wouldn't he drive to his meeting like a normal person?

Because he's meeting someone he shouldn't be, that's why. The question is, who?

The last time I was here was the night of the Scarlet Slippers. Max has made some changes since then. There's an Aztec rug on the floor and a couple of wooden masks on the walls – trophies from his adventures I suppose. In place of the Popovs' display cabinet is a pile of small suitcases, probably packed ready for every kind of international emergency.

Unchanged are Madame's desk and the grand-father clock in the corner. I open the door of the clock case and listen – down below, footsteps clank on the steel treads that lead to the tunnels.

Slipping off my shoes so as not to make a sound, I follow Max into the darkness.

I wind my way down the staircase, clinging on to the handrail. I daren't use the light from the drone in case Max sees it. My tummy bubbles with excitement – every step is taking me closer to proving that Max isn't the hero everyone thinks he is.

When my feet finally find the ground, I take a breath of damp, musty air and listen again.

Music echoes down the tunnel. Max is whistling that same soppy tune. My hand feels the rough stone wall as the sound guides me left, then right. Max passes the tunnel that leads to Meekes and hurries on into the unknown.

I don't notice the flashing light on my wrist until I wipe my forehead. Someone has chosen a very inconvenient time to call.

I stop dead and pant into my Swanphone.

'Who's this?' says the voice on the other end.

'Excuse me,' I puff. 'Shouldn't I be asking that question?'

'Oh, it *is* you, Kydd.'

'*Merv?* What is it? I'm in the middle of a very important mission, remember?'

'No you're not. You're following Max Deverall and breaking every rule in the book while you're at it.'

'I know what I'm doing. If you've called to give me a lecture, you can—'

'I called because you're in trouble. I think Jada Gayle saw you going into Max's study just now.'

My stomach sinks. 'Are you sure? I didn't see anyone.'

'She's the head girl, Kydd – she's good at not being seen.'

Drat. If Jada tells Max I've been in his room, he'll guess that I'm on to him.

'You've got to get back. Now.'

I do a Merv and have a little argument with myself. If I carry on I'll see who Max is meeting, but if I turn around I can find Jada and beg her not to tell.

'*Nooo-kaaay.* I'll be as quick as I can.'

In the distance, Max squeezes through a chink of light. Huffing quietly, I race back the way I came.

I step back into Max's study, expecting to feel Jada's hand on my shoulder, but she must be waiting outside. Maybe there's time for a quick snoop? Max's desk drawer is empty, but I know from last term the drawer isn't what it seems . . . The false bottom comes away easily. Inside are a dozen passports, all with different names and nationalities. But more baffling are the magazines hidden underneath them. Why would Max Deverall have subsciptions to *Gardener's Allotment Monthly* and *Fly Fishing for*

Beginners? Am I missing something? Are they clues? If they are, I'm more clueless than ever.

No sign of Jada out in the corridor. With any luck, she's gone to the refectory with everyone else.

'Over here, Milky Bar!' calls Spencer from one of the tables.

'Have you seen Jada Gayle?' I ask, throwing my bag under an empty chair.

Lottie looks up from her spaghetti. 'No, but Leonora's lookin' for you. Where've you been this time?'

'Sorry, Lottie, as soon as I've found Jada I'll expl—'

I jump so hard, Lottie's spaghetti slithers out of her bowl on to the starched white tablecloth. There's a hand on my shoulder, but it doesn't belong to the head girl. It's the weight of a small boulder.

'You've got some explaining to do, Kydd,' says the Captain, laying a second boulder on my other shoulder. 'Come with us.'

He frogmarches me to Max's study. From all the muttering behind me, I'd say half the refectory is coming too.

It's just as crowded inside. Five stony faces look my way.

Ms Celia's forehead creases as Jada whispers something to Max and Leonora.

Merv's monobrow says, *I told you so*.

Lottie ignores the thundercloud hanging over the Captain's head and elbows her way through the door. 'What's goin' on?'

'I'll tell you what's going on.' The Captain's eyes flash in my direction and I prepare myself for a lightning strike. 'Kydd here has broken Rule Three of *The Guide to Espionage*.'

'What's that?' I ask.

The Captain ignores Leonora's raised hand. 'If you're idiotic enough to break the rules, don't get caught.'

Lottie hooks her arm through mine. 'Milly ain't broken no rules.'

Thanks Lottie.

'Yes she has, she broke into Max's study,' says Jada.

Thanks Jada.

'She what?' Lottie drops my arm.

'I saw her.'

'I can only assume we've got you to thank for unlocking the door.' The Captain aims a lightning bolt right between Merv's eyes. Merv opens his mouth to protest but I aim another one straight at his monobrow. 'What were you thinking, Kydd?'

Max smiles. 'Go easy on her, Captain. I'm sure there's a perfectly good reason.'

'If there is I'd like to hear it,' says Ms Celia.

'Er . . . it's a bit of a long story.'

'Then you'd better get on with it,' says the Captain.

I take a huge breath. This is it. My chance to expose Max and Leonora for the traitors they are. But with everyone staring at me like I'm some kind of exhibit, my words come out in a bit of a jumble.

'Well. It all started when Max saved Bab from the fireworks and left Meekes without a Viennese whirl and Mr Stubbs said jokers don't change their spots, then I heard him on the phone arranging a secret rendezvous, which as you can imagine, made me deeply suspicious when Leonora solved the riddle and found the Nutcracker in my clock, and that's why I followed him into the tunnels.'

'Do you know what she's talking about?' says the Captain to Ms Celia.

Ms Celia shakes her head. 'I think she said Max arranged a secret rendezvous.'

'He did!' I say with an unintended hop. 'Merv made me come back before I saw who he was meeting.'

Merv groans.

'Well, Max?' says Ms Celia.

Max smiles his superstar smile. 'The part about the phone's true. I was organizing a surprise for Leo's birthday. I always use my private phone for private business.'

'And the secret rendezvous?'

'I hate to say it, but that part's a lie. I think she's just being overzealous. And there's probably a little jealousy there too – you know what teenage girls are like. But I get it, Milly – I really do. After everything that happened last term, who wouldn't feel paranoid?'

I can't believe my ears. 'So where *were* you when I was in your room?'

'I was on the other side of the clock, fixing the pendulum. It got broken last term.'

My cheeks burn red hot. 'That's a lie! Max has got something to do with the Mouse King and Leonora's helping him! That's what I was trying to tell you,' I say to Lottie. 'That's what I've been trying to tell you since we got here!'

Max drops the smile. 'Too right I've got something to do with the Mouse King! I've been trying to find him for the last two months.'

'Leo – it ain't true, is it?' asks Lottie, turning from me to Leonora.

'Of course not!' Leonora's eyes are burning as brightly as her dad's. 'That's the most STUPID thing I ever heard. We've given everything to Swan House. There's no way we'd hook up with the Mouse King.'

Words are forming a traffic jam in my throat. They all crash into Lottie. 'You're going to believe her, not me?'

'There's no need to get angry with Lottie,' says Leonora.

'Shut up, Leonora!' I say, flapping my arms at Lottie. 'Can't you see? She's too good to be true! And I bet Nora's not all she was cracked up to be either. You don't even know how she died. She was probably a traitor like them!'

'You've gone too far there, Milly,' says Lottie quietly.

'I agree. That's quite enough.' Miss Celia rests a hand on Leonora's shoulder. 'Milly – I think Max is right. Last term obviously took its toll. I'm aware I was partially to blame for that. If you apologize to Max and Leonora now, we'll forget this ever happened.'

I fold my arms. If the Deveralls think I'm going to let this go, they can think again. 'Sorry for what I said, *about Nora.*'

A vein throbs in Ms Celia's forehead. 'I understand why you might feel a little paranoid. But we all have to move on. We've got far more pressing things to worry about right now. So let's say no more about it. Chop, chop, everyone, we all have classes to attend.'

'Uh, one more thing before she goes,' says Max. 'My drawer had been opened. You didn't take anything did you, Milly?'

'Of course not.'

'Then you won't mind if Jada searches you, just a formality.'

Every nerve in my body jangles as Jada pats me down. She checks inside my shoes. My mouth. My ears. And shakes her head.

'Nothing.'

On the other side of the door, dozens of staring eyes follow me down the corridor. I cross my fingers and hope my backpack is still on the floor where I left it.

Back in the refectory, I find my bag and look for the drone. I unzip the inner pockets, the outer pockets, peer under the table, the chairs, the napkins. I look under Cook's silver domes and behind the counter.

But the drone has gone.

17

The Swancode

'What are you looking for?'

I jump. The problem with spies is they're way too good at sneaking up on you.

Jada's dark eyes are deeply disapproving.

'Er, nothing.'

'I'm watching you, girl. Max might be a nice guy, but I've got your number. Now get to class before you make more trouble.'

I take one last glance around the refectory before leaving. Who took the drone and how am I going to get it back? Just one more problem I can do without. I pause outside the Captain's classroom door before peering inside. I suppose everyone will know what just happened in Max's study . . .

Shoulders back, Milly. Chin out. You know who's right.

I wait for a boo, a well-aimed satsuma, but the class is quiet. Lottie and Supergirl are both reading textbooks – the real sort made with paper and glue. Or at least, they're pretending to be reading. Lottie's book is upside down.

And then I see why. Mr Brown and his clipboard are sitting at the back. Just my luck, the only spare seat is next to him.

The Captain's classroom has had a makeover. The walls are covered in maps and there's a large globe sitting on his desk. In case we hadn't noticed the inspector, the Captain's writing, GEOGRAPHY WITH MR THURGOOD on the whiteboard in extra-large capital letters.

The Captain's had a makeover too. He's squeezed into his jacket and tie and he's combed his beard. But his frown is as deep as the lake.

I slump between the inspector and Spencer. A pen bounces off my shoulder.

'What were you thinking, Kydd?' whispers Spencer.

It's not the first time someone's asked me that today and to be honest, I don't know what I'm thinking myself half the time. In twenty-four hours I seem to have lost Lottie, the compact drone and the trust of half of the school.

The Captain spins the globe and points at a green blob in the middle. 'Today we'll be looking at the terrain of the Casovan mountains. Some of you'll remember the "school trip" we did to Eastern Europe in year seven?'

Mr Brown coughs quietly. 'Aren't we forgetting afternoon registration, Mr Thurgood?'

The Captain narrows his eyes. 'Everyone here?'

The class shouts, 'Yes.'

'Good,' says the Captain. 'So let's get on with it . . .'

Mr Brown coughs again. 'And don't you think you should introduce me to your pupils?'

'No,' says the Captain.

Mr Brown scrapes back his chair. 'In that case, I will introduce myself. Children, I am Mr Brown, and I am here to ensure that your academic, cultural, social and moral needs are being met. Over the coming days, I will observe your lessons, visit your boarding houses and examine your work. I would like to stress that my door is open to any child who feels that the school is falling short in any of the aforementioned categor—'

The Captain begins to rumble.

Mr Brown hugs his clipboard. 'Where did you say you studied to be a teacher?'

'I didn't,' says the Captain.

'*Un-co-op-erative,*' writes Mr Brown and sits down. 'You may continue, Mr Thurgood – Eastern Europe, did you say?'

'Aye, you heard.'

'A rather unusual destination for a school trip, wouldn't you agree?'

'Not if you're a ballet dancer. The children were performing in Moscow, Prague and Sofia. All have a strong tradition in ballet. Now, can I go on?'

With a twitch of his moustache, Mr Brown nods.

'Good. As I was saying, Casova is bound on the east and south by its natural borders, the Casovan mountain range is . . .'

The Captain's only dragged out his old notes on Casova for Mr Brown's benefit. I notice Fleur doze off across the classroom and let my mind wander. Where did that tunnel lead to? Who was Max meeting? Could it have been the Mouse King himself?

By the end of the lesson, I've asked myself a zillion questions and still have no answers. As Lottie and Leonora leave arm in arm, I head back to the refectory for one more search.

'Is this what you're looking for?'

Something gold and round gleams in Bumble's hand. She waves my drone under my nose and slips it in her pocket.

'Give it back!'

'Why should I? It's not yours – I saw Tom Garrick with it last term. It's a doobrie, isn't it?'

'It's just a boring old torch. Tom gave it to me for helping him out.'

'Whatever. Milly, I'm on your side, you know. I don't like the Deveralls any more than you do. If we work together, we could both get what we want.'

'What do you mean?'

'You want Lottie back, don't you?'

'Maybe. And I suppose you want the Sugar Plum Fairy solo.'

Bumble fiddles with her hair. 'That's right. Help me and you might get your doobrie back too.'

'How am I going to do that?'

'I don't know yet, but you can hang out with me while I think of something.'

Bumble barges Spencer's shoulder as she swans out.

'What did she want?'

I explain about the drone. 'I know she's awful, but right now she's the only one who doesn't worship the Deveralls.' I glance up at the hidden cameras. 'I think we'd better talk somewhere else.'

Outside, angry clouds scud across the sky. I wrap my hoody around me as a roll of thunder chases us across the courtyard.

'You and Bumble aren't the only ones who don't

like Max Deverall,' says Spencer, ducking behind the stable block. 'Max broke the rules of fencing. If he can break one set of rules, who's to say he can't break another?'

'I thought you said rules were *meant* to be broken.' I lean against the wall out of the wind.

'There are rules and rules – a gentleman knows the difference. Do you really think Max might be connected to the Mouse King?'

Hail begins to ping off my shoulders. 'Max and Leonora were at the Royal Opera House on the night of the fireworks, and they could have easily planted the Nutcracker doll in my house. Plus he used our trip to Meekes as an excuse to go off somewhere and now he's lied about his rendezvous in the tunnels – I found something weird in Max's desk too – gardening and fishing magazines. He's definitely plotting something. What do you think he's up to?'

'Allotments?' Spencer shrugs. 'Not a clue, but listen, I've been in the library doing a little detective work myself. Thing is, I keep getting referred to the same book, but it's classified.'

'What's it called?' I ask.

'*The Secrets of Swan House, Ancient and Modern.*'

My eyebrows shoot up. 'By Lord Astus? I've seen that book. It's the most highly classified and dangerous book in the school library.'

'How come you've seen it then?'

I peek around the corner, but there's no one around – everyone's inside in the warm and dry. 'It's one of the books Tom Garrick filmed with the drone.'

'OK, that settles it. We're breaking into the library tonight.'

'There are two problems with that, Spence.' I raise my voice as the hail bounces off the stable roof. 'First, Bumble's got the drone and we can't get into the library without it. And second, even if we did find the book, it's written in code.'

'I'll speak to Bumble. Leave it to me.'

'But what about the code?'

Spencer pulls up his hood. 'We'll figure that out when we get there.'

I listen to Leonora's breath, slow and steady. She might be asleep, she might not – slow and steady is how she always breathes.

I slip on my trainers and tiptoe to the door.

'Where are you going?' Leonora opens her eyes. 'Is there something wrong?'

I clutch my stomach. 'I need to get a painkiller off Nurse.'

I score myself an eight out ten on the fib-o-meter. Leonora nods and rolls over. Guess I'm getting better at the whole lying thing.

A figure is waiting in the shadow of the arch. Spencer's teeth chatter over the hoot of a distant owl. 'C-come on, Milky Bar, we haven't got all night.'

A light from Ms Celia's apartment above the coach house casts a yellow glow on the cobbles. 'Extra quiet,' whispers Spencer. 'She's awake.'

We creep across the silent refectory and end up in the lobby. The dark is as thick as Cook's gravy. I trip on the first step and yelp.

Someone snorts behind me. I turn – *Bumble*? I glance accusingly at Spencer.

Bumble holds out the drone. 'I told Spencer – no me, no drone. Here. You can have it back. It really is a boring old torch.'

Spencer brings a finger to his lips. 'Quiet, both of you. This way.'

I climb the stairs with the compact nestled safely in my hand. On my command, it unfolds into a drone. Bumble's upside-down smile vanishes as it purrs along the corridor.

'Open the common room,' I whisper, half expecting an alarm to go off.

The door clicks and Spencer gives me a thumbs up. Once we're inside I order the drone to open the

Virtual Library. My heart skips as the walls begin to shimmer and Sid peers down from her ladder.

'What are you three doin' here?'

'We've come to look at a book,' says Spencer.

Sid sniffs. 'I didnae think ye were here for a swim. What was it ye were lookin' for?'

'*The Secrets of Swan House, Ancient and Modern* by Lord Astus.'

Sid's eyes narrow behind her glasses. 'Yer not the first people to ask for that book tonight.'

I exchange looks with Spencer. 'You mean someone's already borrowed it?'

'Nae borrowed. *Removed.*'

'Removed?' says Bumble. 'What does that mean?'

'Did someone destroy it?' asks Spencer.

'He doesnae listen, does he?' says Sid to me. 'If it'd been destroyed I would ha' said "destroyed".'

'Well, who "removed" it?' asks Spencer.

'I cannae tell you that.'

'But we've got clearance,' I say, remembering what Tom said about the drone.

'Makes nae difference. I cannae tell you who removed it cos I dinnae know. The wee good-for-nothin' disabled me.'

'Disabled you?'

'Aye, hacked the system and turned me off.'

Spencer whispers to me. 'Only a handful of

'people could do that.'

'Max,' I blurt.

'Or Leonora,' says Bumble. 'She's got an IQ of a hundred and forty-nine.'

'Doesn't make sense,' says Spencer. 'If Max wanted the book, with his clearance he could just borrow it.'

'Unless he didn't want anyone to know,' I say.

Spencer gazes up at the drone. 'Wait a minute, didn't you say Garrick filmed the book?'

'Yes, but only part of it, and like I said, all the text is in code.'

'Let's see,' says Bumble.

The drone settles back in my hand and I flip back to mirror mode. 'Show film,' I say.

Spencer and Bumble huddle closer as I fast-forward to Tom opening *The Secrets of Swan House*. I pause it on the floor pattern.

'Do you know what it reminds me of?' Bumble hums a familiar tune, and starts twirling around the tables in a wide circle.

'"Dance of Sugar Plum Fairy"?' says Spencer.

'I suppose it could be the *manège*,' I say. 'But why is it in Lord Astus's book?'

Bumble stops dancing and crashes into me with a giggle. 'Oops. Soooo dizzy!'

Spencer shakes his head and reads the encoded

title. '*NSKA BLCN BSRE.* Any ideas what that means?'

A voice rumbles at the back of my memory. 'Ooo, I totally forgot! The Captain saw the code in my notebook and thought I'd written it. He told me what kind of code it is.'

'Great! So what is it, Milky Bar?'

'Um,' I twiddle my ear. 'Er,' I close my eyes. 'Sorry, I can't remember.'

Spencer groans.

'Let me see that,' says Bumble, still swaying. 'I've been swotting up since Leonora cracked the riddle. I'm not going to let her be the best at everything.' She squints at the page and her eyes light up. 'It's Swancode, look . . .'

Bumble picks up a stray pen from one of the tables and writes out the alphabet on her arm. Then underneath, she writes another alphabet, only this one doesn't start with A, B, C, D. It starts with S, W, A, N. She completes the alphabet, leaving out the letters that make up the codeword.

'I get it,' says Spencer. 'In Swancode, S equals A, W equals B, A equals C, N equals D, B equals E—'

'Exactly, so the title is . . .' Bumble scratches the code on the back of her hand. Underneath that, she writes the corresponding letter of the alphabet. Her eyes glitter with excitement. 'Got it!'

She holds out her hand and Spencer and I both shrug.

NSKA BLCN BSRE
DANC EOFD EATH

'Clear as mud,' says Spencer.

Bumble sighs. 'Swancode's written in four-letter blocks to make it harder for losers like you to decode.'

I take a gulp. That means the blood-red ink spells out, *Dance of Death*.

'I still don't get it,' says Spencer. 'What's Sugar Plum's *manège* got to do with the Dance of Death?'

Bumble pockets the pen. 'Who knows, but it was Max's idea to rehearse *The Nutcracker* this term and I don't believe in coincidences.'

'Neither do I,' says Spencer. 'Rule Thirty-one of *The Guide to Espionage*: Only fools and traitors blame coincidence. The floor pattern has to be worth looking into – we need to carry on searching the library. I'll go through the classified section and you two find every book that mentions the Mouse King.'

Sid pushes up her glasses and points at one of the bookcases. 'Ye'll find him referenced in hundreds of wee books about *The Nutcracker*.'

Five minutes later Bumble and I have a wobbling virtual tower in front of us.

'But these are mostly for kids,' says Bumble. 'I want to read the secret ones with Spencer.'

'I'm not reading for pleasure, you know,' says Spencer, looking up from his book. 'I'm doing my duty in the interests of national security.'

'Really?' says Bumble. 'And what book have you got there – "in the interests of national security"?'

'Just a manual . . .' He sits down. 'Actually, it's really cool. Look, it's got everything you need to know about convertibles.'

'As in cars?' I say. 'What's so secret about them?'

'Not ordinary convertibles, Milky Bar. Look.'

He shows me a picture of a car. It's underwater. It's got fins.

'They're all cars that "convert" into cool things, like Winifred. Can I borrow this, Sid?'

'As long as ye return it within twenty-four hoors.'

'I'll take a book on riddles, I like riddles,' says Bumble.

'OK, and I'll take this,' I say, pointing at the book on the top of my pile. 'It's er,' I read the title. Actually, it's not even a book, it's a collection of newspaper articles called *Twentieth-century Pranks that Turned into Tragedy*.

'Oh. Maybe not that one.'

'Are ye sure?' says Sid. 'The last person to borrow it was Trevor Toppin'.'

Little goosebumps run up my arms. 'When? When did he borrow it?'

'The week before he died.'

'I'll take it.' I check my Swanphone. 'Flying tutus. We've been ages. If Leonora wakes up again and sees I'm not there, she's bound to tell Max. Let's go.'

When we reach the courtyard, Spencer catches Bumble's arm. 'You'd better keep our visit to the library to yourself.'

Bumble tugs away. 'Or what, Spencer? I'm not scared of you or her.' Her eyes flash at me. 'Anyway, why would I say anything? Duh. I'd only get into trouble too—'

'Shh,' I say. From the other side of the arch, the sound of footsteps taps along the cobbles.

We back into the shadows and Spencer peers around the corner. 'It's Brown,' he whispers.

'What's he doing?' I ask.

'What does it look like?' says Bumble. 'He's checking we're all tucked up in bed like good little boys and girls.'

We all watch Mr Brown sniff the night air.

Spencer crouches down and scoops a handful of gravel. 'We can't let him see us. When I give the word – run back to your dorms.'

He leans back and throws the gravel. It soars over the courtyard and rains down on the path leading to the playing fields. Mr Brown stops in his tracks, then scuttles after the noise.

I don't wait for Spencer's word. I bomb across the courtyard, fall into the dorm, dive into bed and heave huge muffled breaths under the covers.

'Where've you been?'

I peep out of the blanket and Lottie's eyes glint in my direction. There's a Leonora-shaped lump in the other bed. Is she awake? Probably.

'Can't say.'

Lottie puffs out. 'Can't or won't? Why are you keepin' secrets, Milly? You know you got Leonora all wrong, and you should never have said that stuff about her mum. What's got into you?'

'You're the one who's got Leonora wrong. The Deveralls are— '

Leonora stirs. 'Is something the matter?'

'Oh, never mind.'

I thump my pillow and Lottie thumps hers. Then we both pretend to fall asleep.

18

There's No Such Thing as Coincidence

While the sun is rising the next morning, I grab my hot-water bottle Boris and creep into the bathroom. Then I sit on the loo and order my Swanphone to open my virtual library book.

The title glows on my lap – *Twentieth-century Pranks that Turned into Tragedy*. I skim through the contents page. Nothing about the Mouse King, so why did Trevor borrow it all those years ago? Then a word catches my eye . . . *Firework*.

I tell the book to open to page twenty-two.

Boy Found Innocent of Arson in Firework Prank That Went Tragically Wrong

Thirteen-year-old Mungoe Thiske of North London has been found innocent of arson in the Bonfire Night prank that killed his parents. Mungoe, known affectionately as 'Mouse' due to his quiet nature, had posted a sparkler through the letterbox of his home while his parents were asleep. Both Kingsley and Florence Thiske were shiftworkers at the ARC Munitions Factory and did not wake up before the blaze took hold. The inquiry discarded the evidence of the boy's friend, Nigel Fletcher, as unreliable. Fletcher, age twelve, claimed that as the house blazed, Thiske had said his parents never saw the funny side of anything, and now the joke was on them. Fletcher later said to reporters, 'Mungoe says I can't call him Mouse any more. He says he's the "Mouse King". I don't think I want to play with his Meccano again.'

I shiver and turn off the book. Could it be a coincidence, or are Bumble and Spencer right and there's no such thing?

Hugging my hot-water bottle Boris, I whisper into my Swanphone. 'Search database for Mungoe Thiske.'

'Sorry Milly, there is no one of that name on our database.'

'Is there somewhere else you can search?'

'The General Register Office may have the records you need. Would you like me to search those?'

'Yes please.'

'Sorry Milly, I have searched births, marriages and deaths, and there is no record of Mungoe Thiske in the national database.'

Drat.

Could Mungoe Thiske have changed his name? Could he have wiped it from the records? Could he be the key to everything?

For the next few days I trudge between classes with heavy legs and a heavier heart. Neither Spencer nor I can find anything related to Mungoe Thiske. As far as the records are concerned, he never existed. On the weekend I try to talk to Lottie, but she's superglued to her new best friend from dawn till dusk. To make matters worse, now that we're partners in crime, Bumble seems to think she's found a new best friend too. Since we broke into the virtual library, she's been following me around like a rottweiler puppy.

I sigh. All through this morning's break, she's been at my side reeling off riddles.

'Did you hear me?' she says. 'What am I?'

'Sorry, Bumble, I wasn't listening. Anyway, I said I was bad at riddles.'

She huffs and gets up. 'OK, maybe you'll listen to this.'

She plonks herself down at the piano. On the other side of the studio, Leonora and Lottie put their hands over their ears.

I cringe as Bumble bashes out a one-fingered

version of 'Dance of the Sugar Plum Fairy'.

'Amy Bee! G-get away from my p-piano!'

Miss Batty charges through the door and drops the piano lid with a clang. Bumble is so surprised she actually does what she's told for once.

She joins me and Spencer at the barre and imitates Miss Batty's stammer behind her back.

'Don't,' I say. 'Miss Batty's usually so sweet, it's not fair to tease.'

'She nearly snapped my head off, and my fingers too,' says Bumble, rubbing the faintest trace of ink on her hand. 'And did you see how fast she was?'

Max claps for our attention. 'OK, people, break over. Let's carry on with the the work we've been doing on the Dance of the Sugar Plum Fairy. Specifically, the trickiest section – the *manège*.'

Bumble smiles her upside-down smile. 'The Dance of Death.'

'Keep your voice down,' says Spencer.

'Hey Spencer!' shouts Max. 'Want to share what's so important? Actually, as you seem to know everything, you can remind everyone what a *manège* is.'

Spencer's jaw twitches. 'It's dancing in a circular pattern around the stage.'

'It's difficult, right?'

Spencer nods.

'But audiences love them, don't they? So girls, the *piqué manège* in the Nutcracker is exceptionally tough. It takes a head-spinning thirty-two counts to complete. You all know how crucial spotting is in executing fast turns, right? Well, in the *manège*, you'll have to change your spot four or five times or you won't know where you are.'

Thirty-two counts? I stretch my leg in front of me and glance at Leonora. She's shaking out her hands, but her shoulders look frozen. Is Leonora Deverall nervous?

'Leonora, Amy, Milly – let's get started. I want to see some beautiful *piqué* turns and a nice crisp finish.'

Max taps his feet. 'Janet, have you got the page? OK. One, two, three, four . . .'

The music begins to tinkle. I go *en pointe* and start to twirl.

One *piqué* . . .

Two *piqués* . . .

Three *piqués* . . .

Leonora's a blur on my left.

Bumble's a blur on my right.

Spot Milly, spot.

'Stop,' says Max.

Puffing hard, I wait for him to lecture me, but he turns to Leonora. 'Leo, you switched your spot in the middle of the double *pirouette* – that's asking for trouble. Next time, change it at the beginning of one of the easier steps. OK, again!'

This time, I really listen to the music. My arms flow, my legs fly, my feet point, but I can't keep it up. My muscles are tired. On the last beat, I lose my balance and come down hard on my heels.

Next to me, Bumble holds her position. Teeth gritted, eyes on Max, she wills him to notice her.

'No, Leo!' says Max. 'What did I say I wanted?'

'A crisp finish,' pants Leonora.

'So what happened? You need to deepen your *plié* before the final step to slow your momentum. When you do the step-up turn, engage your left side. Your turnout will help to put the brakes on.' He adds quietly. 'Blow that and it's game over. OK, everyone, let's call it a day. Same time tomorrow.'

Bumble's hands fall to her hips. 'It's obvious he's already chosen his precious daughter to dance the part.'

'You're right,' I say. 'Sorry, Bumble. You were brilliant.'

Bumble smiles the right way round. 'Thanks.'

Spencer yawns. 'At least you've been rehearsing *something*. So much for us all having a part to play. He hasn't even started the male solos yet.' He shakes his head. 'There must be a connection between the floor pattern, the Mouse King and the Deveralls, but what is it?'

Out in the lobby, I catch Lottie's eye and try to smile. She makes her way over without smiling back.

'I fought I knew you better, Milly. You're lettin' Bumble follow you around like a bad smell.'

'Excuse me girls.' We both step back as Mr Brown makes his way to the theatre. My smile fades and I glare at Leonora. 'You can talk. At least Bumble isn't trying to pretend to be something she's not.'

'Leo ain't pretendin'.'

Lottie spins around as a gust of wind blasts through the lobby. A bright pink nose pokes through the entrance. 'Pssst, Billy!'

Topsy beckons me nearer.

'Just a second.' I turn to ask Lottie to wait, but she's already gone. A weight like a cold hot-water bottle presses on my chest.

'Pssst,' says Topsy again.

'What is it?' I snap.

'Is Bister Brown there? He's been lookig for be but I've got a top secret visitor out here, ad Bizz Celia says I've got to get hib to her study without beig seen . . . like a proper spy!'

'It's OK, the coast is clear. Mr Brown just went to the theatre.'

Topsy backs through the entrance and I rush to hold the door. She's trying to manoeuvre an exceed-ingly old man in a wheelchair. He's wearing a moss-green moleskin jacket with patches on the elbows and old shoes, shiny as conkers.

He smiles and I smile back. I like old people, especially when they're not talking about trout. This one doesn't look like the fishing sort. He slides his glasses up his nose. There's nothing old about the cat-green eyes behind them.

Topsy spins the wheelchair around. '*Eek*. It's Bister Brown!'

Uh-oh. Mr Brown and his clipboard have emerged from the theatre and are scurrying down the corridor towards us. His moustache is twitching in irritation.

'Miss Topping. Miss Topping! I've been looking for you everywhere . . .'

Topsy starts to back out.

'Wait,' I say, feeling bad for snapping. 'I can take Ms Celia's visitor.'

'Oh, would you, Billy? JUST A BINIT BISTER BROWN! Take hib to the director's lift, please-thank-you. Bizz Celia's waitig upstairs.'

'The director's lift? Where's that?'

'In the yoga roob, on the right.'

As Topsy leads Mr Brown back towards the theatre, the old man holds out his hand. His palm is ice-cold, despite the woolly blanket tucked around his knees. I give it a gentle shake and introduce myself.

'Milly Kydd. Well, well, well.' His voice is light

and airy, like it's walking on its tiptoes. 'I knew your mother – Eva was an extraordinary talent. But let's not talk here, we'd better hurry before the school inspector returns.'

I take Topsy's place behind the wheelchair and whizz down the corridor. As we screech into the yoga room, my passenger makes a sound like a car on a frosty morning.

'Sorry, was that too fast?'

His shoulders shake and I realize he's not choking, he's laughing.

'Don't be sorry. It's been a long time since I moved like that. Between you and me, I loved fast cars when I was a boy. Speed makes me feel young again.'

The yoga room is on the ground floor of the octagon. Sunlight pours through the windows and dances across the spidery veins on the old man's cheeks. I search each of its eight walls for the lift.

'The lift is disguised in the wood panelling,' he says. 'I installed it back in the seventies. I was younger back then, of course – too vain to think I'd have to use it myself one day. Old age doesn't come alone, Milly.'

I nod like I know what he means and push the chair closer to the panelling. 'I can't see any buttons.'

'That's because it's voice activated.' He clears his throat. 'Would you be so kind as to open, lift.'

One of the wall panels slides smoothly away, revealing an old-fashioned lift. I push the chair inside and jump as a voice from above us shrieks.

'Darling! It's been too long. Where can I take you?'

'Straight to the director, please.' The old man smiles at my startled face in the lift mirror. 'She's fun, isn't she? I used the voice of a prima ballerina friend of mine. Terrible diva, but heart of gold.'

'Do behave, or I won't budge,' giggles the diva-lift, who's beginning to remind me of Bab.

Before I've noticed we're moving, the doors slide open again and we're face to face with Ms Celia.

She takes control of the wheelchair. 'Thank you, Milly, I'll take over now. Hugo, thank you so much for coming. As I said on the phone, we have a small puzzle— Milly, you can go for lunch now. Lift, please take her down to the ground floor.'

A puzzle?

As we go down, I realize the old man didn't tell me his name. When I ask the lift it sighs.

'Why, that's Hugo Kinsmeet, darling. He's one in a zillion.'

In the dorm that night, I listen while Leonora and Lottie talk about Ms Celia's visitor.

'Mr Kinsmeet didn't like Dad when he was in school – he was always blaming him for things.'

I'm not surprised. Mr Stubbs said Max was a terror.

'Dad said he made cool doobries though.'

I smile to myself – I've got two of them in the music box under my bed.

Lottie's eyes widen. 'Like what?'

'Dad didn't get to use most of them. I think that's why he likes to collect old doobries now.'

'Nora might've though,' says Lottie. 'Let's ask her what they was.'

I blurt out, 'The Captain said no mentors, Lottie. Not until the inspector's gone. And they'll know you've switched her on.'

'Brown'll be countin' sheep by now – you just don't want Leo to see Nora.'

Leonora pipes up. 'And that's not very nice, Milly.'

Grrr.

Seconds later, Nora Doone is perched at the end of Lottie's bed like a dainty lilac bird. Wish I could conjure up my mum whenever I felt like it. But before she says a word, our Swanphones begin to flash.

'Told you we'd be in trouble,' I say.

Leonora sighs. 'Sorry, Lottie – I'll tell the Captain it was my fault.'

Lottie grins. 'You won't have to. This ain't got nuffink to do wiv Nora.'

She reads out the message. 'FAO all students. Make your way immediately to the coach house. Do not make a sound. It is imperative that Mr Brown is not disturbed. Flamin' Nora – no offence, Nora. Ms Celia's declared a flippin' Code Pink!'

19

The Code Pink

Outside, the moon plays peek-a-boo behind the clouds. The carriage lights have been extinguished and dark shapes flit along the walkway. A couple of year sevens shriek and are promptly shushed by William Flynn. The whole school is heading for the coach house.

I follow Lottie and Leonora dipping in and out of the drizzle. The only sounds are the gentle pizzicato of rain and the *thud, thud, thud* of my heart. A Code Pink is the highest level of threat – something awful's happened . . . or is about to happen.

Looks like we're the last to arrive. The Captain presses a finger to his lips and waves us inside the coach house. Checking behind us, he closes the door.

The coach house smells of engine oil, like Ms Celia. Winifred's headlights flood the darkness. Behind the rows of shiny bumpers and excited faces, I spot Ms Celia and Max talking urgently.

The Captain herds us all into a semi-circle around Ms Celia. Spencer and Merv push in front of me. Merv's in his Star Trek pyjamas – a part of me wishes Scotty would beam me up too.

A creak breaks the silence. All eyes turn to the door. I freeze – if it's Mr Brown, we're done for.

The Captain gets there in two Viking strides, but the door's already half open.

A head peers inside.

Madge Little tugs down her nightie. 'Am I late?'

The Captain's shoulders heave.

'Not at all. Come in, Madge,' says Ms Celia quietly. 'I want you to see this.'

Madge is halfway through the door when a second figure hurtles into her back. The Captain grabs the hurtler in a headlock.

There's a squeal. 'HELP BE, SUBONE!'

I double take. The hurtler is a fluffy pink unicorn.

'Oh, sorry, pet,' says the Captain, rearranging the hood of the unicorn's onesie.

'It's all right, Captain,' says Topsy, straightening her horn. 'By fault for beig late.'

There's a snigger from Bumble's direction.

The alarm on Ms Celia's forehead rearranges itself back into worry. When we've all settled down, she steps into Winifred's beam and tightens the cord of her paisley dressing gown.

'Now that we're all here, I must apologize for the setting and the hour. With Mr Brown residing in the suite above the theatre, I didn't think it would be wise to use the school. And I'm afraid the matter couldn't wait until the morning.'

I stamp my feet. The cold from the stone floor is beginning to seep through my slippers.

Ms Celia clears her throat and we all hush.

'As you know, in the early hours of last Wednesday, we recovered a Nutcracker doll from the Kydd household. It appears to be a child's toy, but we suspected its meaning was far from innocent. Its vile purpose eluded us until tonight, when, thanks to the assistance of an old friend of Swan House, we at last managed to unlock the Mouse King's message.'

An old friend? She must mean Hugo Kinsmeet.

Ms Celia delves into her pocket and puts something on Winifred's bonnet. Lottie and I peep over Spencer's shoulder.

The doll looks like a toy soldier. Its scarlet jacket is trimmed with gold, its cap and boots are black. Its face is painted with an ugly grin.

The cold crawls up my calves and along my spine. I glance at Max, but his face is in shadow.

The Nutcracker doll's jaw hangs open. We all edge closer as a tinny little voice echoes around the garage.

'*There was a crooked boy,*
Who played a crooked game,
He danced a crooked dance,
Which failed its crooked aim,
He found a crooked school,
But not the crooked mouse,
Who hid a crooked prize,
In a crooked tower of his house.'

The cackle that follows makes my scalp prickle.

'This time, his meaning is clear,' says Ms Celia gravely. 'The "crooked boy" can only refer to one person; Ivan Korolev.'

Max's old friend, Korolev – it can't be a coincidence!

Ms Celia goes on. 'Korolev once tried to win the Scarlet Slipper Ballet Prize by poisoning the other finalists. Later he went on to found Korolev's Dance Academy, the most "crooked school" in the world. The "crooked tower" refers to one of the four towers in Black Lodge, Korolev's castle in Casov—'

'Ahhhh-TISHOOO!'

Ms Celia's hand flies to her Swanphone.

Topsy blows her nose noisily. 'Bless be! Sorry, Bizz Celia. Just a little cold – please carry on.'

Ms Celia's hand drops shakily to her side. 'As I was saying, the Mouse King is claiming to have hidden a "crooked prize" right under Korolev's nose. A weapon known as the Nutcracker. To make matters worse, our sources tell us that Korolev has received a similar riddle. Once again, the Mouse King is playing a game with Swan House. He is pitting us against our enemies. We have no choice but to go to Korolev's school and find the Nutcracker before he does. Children, activate your mentors. We're going to need all the help we can get.'

Voices murmur in greeting as the mentors glow next to their students – Nora, Dafydd, Han Wu. Everyone stares at Ivan.

'What are you all looking at? He's just an avatar,' snaps Spencer.

Ivan whispers something in his ear.

Next to me, Trevor flickers like a faulty light bulb. 'Greetings, Milly, I rememb—'

'Shh, Trevor, I'm trying to listen to Ivan. What did he say, Spencer?'

'He swears he doesn't know anything about the Nutcracker weapon.'

'What about you, Nora?' asks Lottie.

Nora shakes her head. 'Sorry, Lottie, since this information came to light, there hasn't been enough time to update our systems.'

Trevor is practically hopping from foot to foot. 'Milly . . .'

'What is it, Trevor?'

'The Nuh-uh-oh,' says Trevor before disappearing completely.

He really is the worst mentor ever.

Lottie puts up her hand. 'Ms Celia, what kind of weapon is the Nutcracker?'

Ms Celia slips the doll back in her dressing gown pocket. 'I wish there was a straightforward answer to that question, Lottie, but unfortunately it's rather complicated. For years, we believed the Nutcracker was no more than a myth. Some said it was the smartest weapon on the planet – so smart it could control every weapon system in the world. Some said it was entirely sentient, that it could make decisions for itself, including who should live and die . . .' She trails off. 'But whatever the truth, we are certain that in the wrong hands, the Nutcracker could unleash enormous harm. So, we must find it, retrieve it and destroy it. If we fail, the consequences could be catastrophic.'

Merv is shaking his head like the world is about to end.

Oh help. Maybe it is.

Why would Max want such a horrible weapon? I study Leonora for a twitch of remorse, a guilty blink, but her spy-face is as unreadable as ever.

'One last thing,' says Ms Celia, switching back to her no-nonsense voice. 'Over the coming days, we will choose an elite team to take part in this mission. Given the dangers involved, I will be asking for volunteers. If you wish to sign up, please let the Captain know as you leave. In a moment Max and the Captain will take you through the details.'

'Yes!' says Lottie with a fist pump. 'No more Sugar Plum flippin' Fairy rehearsals. I'm signin' up right now – what about you, Leo?'

Leonora shivers. 'Of course, but it's going to be really dangerous, Lottie. If the Nutcracker is sentient, it has a conscious mind – it can feel and think for itself like we do.'

'So in that case it might have a conscience?' I say, hopefully. 'Maybe it doesn't want to destroy the world?'

Lottie rolls her eyes. 'The clue's in the name, Milly. It's the Nutcracker WEAPON.'

I start shivering too. Someone's got to stop Max and if I don't volunteer, what'll happen to Lottie and the rest of the team in Casova? What will happen to the *world*?

'If Korolev finds it first, we're all DOOMED,' says Merv.

'Don't you ever look on the bright side?' says Spencer.

'There is no bright side.'

Merv jumps as Trevor appears in front of him.

'There's always a bright side, Merv – you just need to cross to the sunnier side of the street.'

'Absolutely,' says Spencer, 'It's an all-expenses-paid trip to Casova. Our first mission of the year.'

Merv shakes his head pityingly. 'And most probably OUR LAST.'

Max lays a hand on his shoulder. 'Korolev's school may be an impenetrable castle overlooking treacherous seas. But, I'm happy to say, there is a glimmer of hope.'

'See,' says Trevor to Merv as he wriggles out of Max's grasp.

Sweeping his coat around him like a cape, Max steps into the beam of Winifred's headlights. 'This won't be the first time I've broken into Korolev's school. I know a route up the cliffs and a weakness in the castle's defences. Leonora's already studied the security system, so she can disable it before we enter.'

'We can all be reassured,' says Ms Celia. 'With both of you on our team, we have every chance of success.'

I shake my head in time with Merv's. No wonder Max sounds so confident. He must have planned this with Korolev. It's some kind of trap!

Max says, 'We also have luck on our side. In four days' time, Korolev's academy are performing for the Casovan president at the Grand Palace. It's our only chance to get into the castle and carry out the search. Tomorrow night, we'll start a programme of intense training.'

'Four days!' exclaims Jada Gayle. 'But what if Korolev finds the Nutcracker before we do?'

'Then we'll just have to fight him for it,' answers the Captain. 'Any more questions?'

Spencer calls out. 'Why did you need help with the doll?'

Ms Celia frowns. 'As it turned out, it could only be unlocked by the voice of our old Shoe Keeper, Hugo Kinsmeet. Obviously, the Mouse King still sees him as a worthy adversary.'

Someone asks how we're going to train with the inspector prowling around, but before the Captain can answer, there's a *thwump* at his side.

'Emmie?' he says, crouching over the furry, pink heap on the floor. He pulls off Topsy's hood. 'Celia, her temperature's through the roof.'

'Take her to the infirmary, quickly, Garth,' says Ms Celia. 'I should have made her see the nurse days ago.'

The Captain scoops up Topsy in his Viking arms and hurries out.

'Quieten down, everyone,' says Max. 'Nurse will take care of Topsy. We have to focus on the job in hand. If you think you're up to it and want to volunteer, see me before you leave.'

'Everyone else may go back to their dorms and rest,' adds Ms Celia. 'This might be your last chance to get a proper night's sleep before the mission.'

Before I can talk myself out of it, I take my place in the queue behind Bumble.

'What are you doin'?' says Lottie.

'Volunteering,' I say, trying not to shake in my slippers.

Leonora gives me one of the smiles she saves for the littlest year sevens. 'That's really brave of you, Milly, but you don't have the experience. I'd go to bed if I were you, get a good night's sleep. You must need it after your tummy ache the other night.'

Bumble turns around. 'Who made *you* in charge of the mission, Leonora? Milly can sign up if she wants to.'

Lottie surprises me by agreeing. 'Course she can. She'll still have to prove herself in trainin', like the rest of us.'

'You're right, Lottie,' says Leonora. 'We all will – Dad'll only choose the best.'

20

The Castle in the Air

Next morning, I yawn all the way to ballet. Even though the volunteers will be training at night with the Captain, we still have to carry on with daytime classes for Mr Brown's benefit. I really need to get some sleep but frankly, sharing a dorm with a potential supervillain makes sleeping impossible.

Snowdrops push up through the frosty lawn, but right now spring feels like it might never come.

Inside the dance studio, wintery sunshine pours through the windows. Bumble is absorbed in a small fire she's made using a mirror and a piece of paper. She calls me over.

'Guess what this is:
It dances just like you and I
Lighting up the darkest sky
Give it food and it will live
Give it water and it will die.
What is it?'

I stamp out the flames. 'You shouldn't play with fire, Bumble.'

'Got your attention though, didn't I? Always works at home too. I'll show you how to do it if you like.'

'No thanks. Where's Max?'

Bumble shrugs.

At the other end of the barre, Spencer sets off a Mexican wave of yawns which reaches me just as Max Deverall bounds through the door.

He claps his hands. 'Wake up, Milly! Mr Brown's on his way, so let's look lively!'

I stifle another yawn and put up my hand. 'Is Topsy going to be OK?'

'Nurse said she's going to be fine. She just needs a rest from you guys. OK, everyone, let's start with a gentle warm-up. Janet, something nice and *adagio*, please.'

As the piano begins to tinkle, the doors swing open.

'Smile, folks,' mouths Max before turning to the inspector. 'Ahh, good morning, Mr Brown.'

Mr Brown drags a chair near the window. 'We shall see about that, Mr Deverall.'

He runs his beady brown eyes around the class and jots something on his clipboard. 'Please carry on, children, just pretend I'm not here.'

'OK, let's stretch out those shoulders and backs,' says Max. 'Open your chests. That's right, breathe everyone. And now into first position.'

Focus, Milly, focus.

We work slowly through our exercises but the sun is radiating a dozy heat that makes it harder and harder to concentrate . . .

'Stop the music.'

Max raises an eyebrow. 'Did you say something, Horace? Can I call you Hor—'

'No you can not,' says Mr Brown. 'I said stop the music.'

Miss Batty's fingers slow to a halt.

'The children are a shambles,' says Mr Brown. 'They look as if they've been awake all night. *That one*,' he says, pointing at me, 'is so behind the music she could be dancing backwards. One would hope to see more vigour and precision in this class, especially given your reputation, Mr Deverall.' Mr Brown scrapes back his chair. 'I hope to see some improvement tomorrow.'

When he's gone, Max calls us to the centre. 'What happened? It's like you'd all forgotten how to dance.'

'That's because this is a waste of time,' says Spencer. 'We should be training for the mission. Someone needs to take care of Brown.'

'What do you suggest, Spencer? A fall on the stairs? A little *poison*?'

'Of course not, I—'

Max's eyes smoulder. 'Mr Brown will leave Swan House in one piece. Until he leaves, we'll make sure his evening cocoa's laced with a drop of Nurse's sleeping draught. And if you can't cope with dancing by day and training by night, maybe you should think again about volunteering?'

Spencer scowls at Max. 'I'll be there, don't worry.'

Later that night, the volunteers crowd silently into the Captain's classroom. I glance from Lottie and Leonora to Bumble and Spencer – nearly all the others are sixth formers. It's going to take a miracle for Max and the Captain to choose me.

Everyone shuffles around a table in the centre of the room. Max points his Swanphone at the tabletop and we all gawp as it begins to shimmer.

'Whoa!' says Lottie as the shimmering turns into a swirling blue-black sea.

'The Casovan Sea,' says Max with satisfaction. 'And this is Black Lodge.'

Virtual cliffs soar up from the waves. Squatting at the top, like a malevolent old crow, is a medieval castle.

'Madge has been working on the hologram for years,' says Max. 'With my help, she's managed to complete an accurate model.'

'The castle is Korolev's family seat,' explains the Captain. 'Originally, it was a hunting lodge graced by kings and cut-throats alike. When Korolev was kicked out of Swan House, he returned home and transformed the castle into an academy of dance.'

Black Lodge is as castley as a virtual castle can be. It has ramparts and parapets, towers and turrets – windows as slitty as the eyes of a little black mole.

Max points at the top of the cliff face. 'We plan to land here.'

'That's impossible,' says Bumble.

'It would be if we didn't have Ms Celia's convertibles.'

Spencer whoops. 'You mean we're going to *fly* there?'

'The five people we *select* will fly there, yes. There will be a team of four in each convertible, including me and the Captain. My team will travel in Earnest, and the Captain's in Winifred.'

'Who's Earnest?' I ask.

'Ms Celia's Reliant Robin.'

Bumble snorts and the Captain frowns. 'Never judge—'

'A car by its bonnet, whatever,' says Bumble. 'You

said five people. Does that mean you've chosen Leonora already?'

'Leonora is vital to the plan,' says Max. 'We'll be relying on her to disable the security system.'

'Bet anyone could do that,' says Bumble.

Max's fingers drum through virtual waves. 'Leonora's going, let's move on. As you can see, the castle has four towers. The Prison Tower, Dance Tower, Weapons Tower and Watch Tower. We'll need to split up and search each one. By the time we enter, Leonora will have switched off the alarms, so it really should be a walk in the park.'

I study the hologram and wonder what kind of parks Max goes to . . . Jurassic?

The floor creaks as the Captain gets to his feet. 'Thank you, Max. We'll meet the same time tomorrow night for a crash course in rock climbing.'

Rock climbing? Lottie's fist pump goes straight through Korolev's castle.

Once we're back in the dorm, I lie awake all night, worrying about Max and Korolev, and castles in the air.

The following night, we meet in the courtyard. The moon hangs over the octagon roof. The Captain gathers us in its deepest, darkest shadow.

'The first thing to remember about rock climbing is not to rush – treat it like a slow dance.'

'An *adagio*, not an *allegro*,' says Max.

The Captain grunts. 'If you want to be all balletic about it, yes.'

With quiet clicks and deft hands, he shows us how to 'prusik up a rope', 'tie off our belay plates' and do all kinds of unpronounceable things with knots. An hour later, I'm climbing up the wall to shouts of, 'Kydd, I said to use your legs not arms, your toes not heels!' Twenty minutes after that, I'm abseiling off the roof. After my experience with Madge's flying tutu, the going down bit's a doddle – this time I've got ropes and everything! When I hit the ground, the Captain says if I could do it without screaming I'd be top of the class.

'Can I do it again?' I ask.

'No time, pet,' says the Captain. 'Tomorrow you've got a lesson with the Shoe Keeper.'

Spencer's grin is as big and cheesy as the moon.

'What are you looking so pleased about?' says Bumble.

'That means we finally get some doobries.'

Bumble's face lights up too. 'Oh yeah, and the weapons on our Swanphones.'

On the way back to the dorm, I hang back with

Spencer. 'Listen, Spence, we have to talk to Ms Celia about Max again. How do we know everything he said about Korolev's castle is true? I think he and Korolev are plotting something when we get there. The mission is dangerous enough as it is. We've got to make Ms Celia believe us.'

Spencer flips up his hood. 'I was thinking the same thing, Milky Bar. Let's talk to her after breakfast. She'll be in her studio.'

I head back to my dorm feeling calmer. With Spencer on my side, Ms Celia's bound to listen.

But I hadn't reckoned on Mr Brown. The rumours start over breakfast. By the time we've finished eating, our worst fears have been confirmed.

On the table behind me, Lottie bangs down her knife. Spencer and I twist in our chairs. 'Brown's done what?' she says. 'He can't close the school – he ain't got the aufority!'

'Oh yes he has,' says Jada Gayle, handing out letters. 'Read it. It's from Ms Celia.'

We all listen as Lottie reads aloud.

'Dear students, the school inspector has seen fit to fail the school on every key area.'

We all gasp.

'In short, this means we must close the school forfwiff.'

We all gasp again.

Lottie scans the next paragraph. 'She's notified our parents and everyfink. It's really happenin'!'

'I'm going to kill Mr Brown,' says Bumble quietly. 'Where is he?'

'Slunk out before breakfast,' says Jada.

'Then I'm going to hunt him down and—'

'Shh, Bumble,' says Leonora, 'Let Lottie finish. What else does the letter say? Surely the work we do here is too important to stop.'

Lottie carries on. 'Your parents will collect you at lunchtime today. Rest assured, this is a temporary measure. I am currently in Westminster attemptin' to meet wiv certain government officials who will no doubt overturn Mr Brown's decision—'

'Ms Celia's gone?' I say weakly.

'Left straight after Brown,' Jada replies.

I frown at Spencer. We were going to talk to her about Max. What are we going to do now?

Lottie sniffs. 'I ain't finished readin' yet . . . *however*, this may take a little time. Regrettably, the closure will have severe consequences for the timetable. As you know, an important school trip had been planned for tomorrow. This will go ahead. If you have been chosen to go, you will receive a notification today. I wish you all a safe journey. Sincerely, Celia Sitwell, DCB.'

Lottie hands me the letter. She's so angry with Mr Brown, she's forgotten to be angry with me. 'I said Brown was a sneak!' Then she remembers and snatches the letter back.

'What do you think Ms Celia meant about the school trip?' I say.

Jada Gayle whispers, 'Ms Celia's decided the mission'll go ahead as planned. She's going to keep back the five volunteers who've been chosen. I'd advise you all to keep an eye on your Swanphones. You'll know by lunchtime.'

Back in the dorm, I open my trunk and begin throwing clothes inside, then I check my Swanphone for the hundredth time. The Captain's got to pick me and Spencer. Who else is going to stop Max and Leonora from doing whatever it is they're planning to do?

But deep down, I know I'm the last person he'll want to take. Let's face it, the mission needs people like Jada Gayle and William Flynn – proper spies who can climb rocks and karate kick with their eyes closed.

I karate kick with my eyes open and still manage to stub my toe on my trunk. Then the lid slams shut and I get a horrible feeling that I've packed up my friendship with Lottie too.

There are voices in the courtyard. 'Of *course* you're coming, Lottie. Dad said after William Flynn, you were his first choice.'

'What about Milly?' says Lottie.

'Milly? She hasn't got any skills.'

I kick my trunk with the other foot.

'Yes she has,' says Lottie. 'And she's brave. As brave as anyone else here. That's got to count for somefink.'

My eyes prickle. Maybe there's hope for our friendship yet?

'I really think Milly's better off at home with Bab,' says Leonora. 'Some jobs should be left to the experts. Oh, look – it's a message about the mission . . .'

My Swanphone flashes.

I read the message under my breath. 'Sorry, Milly, you have not been selected for Operation Nutcracker. Prepare to be collected shortly. Please don't forget to hand me in before you leave the premises.'

Lottie whoops outside.

I read the message again . . . . *You have not been*

196

selected . . . Prepare to be collected. 'Collected'? Collected by who?

Wait a minute, it can't be. Not . . . Mum?

OF COURSE MUM! She said she'd be home soon.

My heart *ballons* and my feet do too. When I tell Mum about Max and the Mouse King, the Deveralls will be taken away, then we'll go to Casova and find the Nutcracker, and the school will reopen, and EVERYTHING WILL BE FINE.

21

A Lesson with the Shoe Keeper

There's a rap on the door.

'Milky Bar, let me in!'

'Coming!' I *ballon* across the dorm.

I can see by Spencer's grin that he's going to Casova.

'You got picked?'

'Yes – thanks to the Captain. Did you?'

'No, but it's OK, Mum's on her way. When I tell her what's happened, she'll . . .' My Swanphone flashes again.

'What is it?' asks Spencer, helping himself to the last of my biscuits.

I read the message and the *ballon* goes out of me. I sink to my trunk. 'She's been delayed for twenty-four hours. That's too late.'

'Don't worry, I can stop the Deveralls.'

'You can't take them on by yourself, Spencer. The Deveralls are superspies. Do you know who else is going?'

'Apart from Li and Leonora, no. Maybe Bumble got picked though? She'd do anything to bring Leonora down. I'll go talk to her. Maybe you should speak to the Captain – see if he'll change his mind.'

The moment Spencer's gone, I video-message the Captain.

'Sorry, pet,' he says. 'The team's been finalized.'

'Captain, you don't understand – I HAVE to go to Casova.'

'Listen, your Mam'll be here soon – better get ready, eh?'

'Mum can't come until tomorrow. Please, Captain—'

'There's nothing I can do. Max wouldn't budge.'

'Max?'

'After your little outburst the other day, he doesn't trust you.'

He doesn't trust *me*? Grrr. 'But—'

'Look, if you've got to stay here, you may as well learn something. Come to Madge Little's lesson.'

I jump up from the trunk. 'OK. Is it in the shoe cupboard? That'll be a bit of a squash.'

'Kydd, I hope you're joking. It's in my classroom.'

'Ha ha, course. I'll be there in a sec.'

All signs of the last lesson have been cleared away. The Captain ushers me in while Madge flits between the tables, handing out industrial-sized earmuffs.

'Boom-cancelling,' she says to me, by way of explanation.

At the front of the class are Lottie and Bumble. They both raise an eyebrow when they see me. Spencer's chatting with William Flynn near the window and the Deveralls are whispering at the back. In the far corner with his head in his hands is Merv. What's he doing here?

'You didn't volunteer, did you?' I say, slumping into the seat next to him.

'Me?' says Merv. 'Volunteer?' His monobrow *jetés*. 'Do you think I've got some kind of death wish?'

'So what are you doing here?'

Merv hrmphs. 'Someone's got to man the CR. And with Ms Celia away, I'm in charge of all comms. How come you're here?'

'Er . . . because the Captain said so?'

Merv hrmphs again.

I look around. If Merv's not going, aren't they one person short? Where's number eight? I unslump as a thought pops into my brain. Maybe I am here for a reason? Maybe the Captain's persuaded Max to take me after all?

The Captain perches on the end of his desk. 'Right, first things first, now that Brown's wriggled back to his little hole, you can activate your mentors again.'

Seconds later, there's a chorus of *Greetings, what can I do for you*s? Merv ducks as Han Wu somersaults over his head. Nora places a graceful hand on the back of Lottie's chair. Trevor bumbles beside mine.

Madge walks right through him and hands me an industrial-sized pair of safety goggles. 'Flame resistant,' she says.

'Thank you, Madge,' says the Captain. 'So, moving on to today's lesson. We know that Leonora can disable the alarm. After that, we'll be relying on our technology to give us the edge over Korolev. That's where your Swanphones come in . . . Kydd, did I tell you to put those on?'

I mumble a sorry and take the goggles off.

'Over to you, Madge,' says the Captain.

Madge Little wrings her small pink hands. 'Oh dear, I forgot to bring the Swansuits.'

'Don't worry about those for now,' says Max from the back of the class. 'Let's concentrate on firepower.'

Firepower?

Who knew there were so many ways of disarming people? To Spencer's delight, our Swanphones can stun, blast, zip, freeze . . . the list goes on. By the time

Madge has finished her demonstration, William Flynn has lost an eyebrow, Bumble has a frozen tongue and I have died of embarrassment. Every time Madge aimed her Swanphone, Trevor insisted on throwing himself in front of me like some sort of human shield.

'Sorry, Milly,' he says, straightening his jumper, 'old habits die hard. I keep forgetting I'm a hologram.'

Next, Madge gives us a utility belt. I peer over Bumble's shoulder as she tips out the contents. A tube of mints, a can of hairspray, a packet of bobby pins, a strawberry lip salve, toothbrush, toothpaste and a small tin of rosin.

'Miss Little,' says Leonora. 'Milly isn't going on the mission. That utility belt should be Jada Gayle's – she'll be here in a minute.'

Madge scratches her guinea-pig hair. 'That's not Jada's, it's an old one fom the back of the cupboard. The Captain told me to bring nine belts, didn't you, Captain?'

'Aye, there's no harm in Kydd learning to handle some doobries while she's here.'

I heave a sigh. Silly Milly. Of course Max hasn't changed his mind. Of course Jada Gayle is going.

'Please don't touch anything until I've finished,' says Madge, picking up the rosin.

Max chuckles. 'Is that good old-fashioned fog powder?'

'That's right. So thick you can't see your own feet,' says Madge.

'A bit like Trevor Topping,' adds Max.

I ignore all the giggles and change the subject. 'And these?' I pick up the mints.

'Wheezer mints. They can alter your voice by up to four octaves.'

Lottie gives the hairspray a shake.

Madge squeaks. '*Don't squirt!* It's pepper spray. Low tech but very efficient at close quarters.'

I know what the bobby pins are. Tom Garrick gave me some lock picks last term. Bumble starts to unscrew the lip salve.

'Put that down.' Madge snatches it away and holds it at arm's length. 'It's got an explosive device in the lid.'

'What are these for?' I ask, gingerly prodding the toothpaste and brush.

Madge frowns. 'Why, healthy teeth and gums, of course.'

There's a creak in the corridor and the Captain leaps up. Jada Gayle backs through the door and pushes a wheelchair to the front of the class.

Its passenger gives me a wink.

'Golly,' says Trevor. 'It's my inventor – now what was his name? It's on the tip of my tongue . . . no, don't tell me . . .'

'Hugo, you came!' says Madge, clapping her hands.

'That's it!' says Trevor. 'Hugo, er, Hugo . . .'

'Hello, Madge. Delighted to be of service,' says Mr Kinsmeet. 'Good Lord.' He unfolds his knobbly hands. 'Isn't that Trevor Topping? My very first avatar.'

'I remember now!' shouts Trevor. 'Hugo *Kinsmeet*! Rule Thirteen, Milly!'

'What's he going on about. Can't you shut him up?' says Bumble.

'Shhh, Trevor,' I hiss between my teeth. 'Do you have to be so embarrassing?'

'I had no idea he was still operating,' says Mr Kinsmeet.

'Only just,' I mutter.

Hugo chuckles. 'And Max Deverall too! You certainly kept me on my toes. How are you, Max?'

Max smiles his superstar smile. 'Very well. I owe you so much.'

'That's very kind. Very kind indeed.'

Madge says. 'Everyone, I've invited Mr Kinsmeet here because he's an expert on the Nutcracker weapon.'

'The N-uh-oh,' says Trevor and pops into nothing.

I sigh and turn to Merv. 'See what I meant about him being broken. Please can't you do something?'

Merv grunts. 'I'll try, but I'm very busy.'

Mr Kinsmeet clears his throat. 'Thank you, Madge. I'm afraid no one knows the weapon's full capabilities, but after many years of study, I can prepare you in part for what you may come up against.'

'Can you start by telling us what we should be looking for?' says the Captain. 'What does the Nutcracker look like and where are we most likely to find it?'

'Of course, Captain. I'm afraid your quest won't be easy. The Nutcracker is not something you can hold in your hands – it is a malicious piece of software which exists merely as lines of code. You must find the hardware on which the malware was originated. This could be a small and insignificant laptop, or the mainframe of a vast computer. Whichever it is must be destroyed immediately.'

Jada raises her hand. 'How will we know when we've found it?'

'Good question, Miss Gayle. Before you leave for Casova, Madge will upgrade your Swanphones with a special sensor.' The old man taps his bony wrist. 'You simply connect your Swanphone with the suspect device, and if the Nutcracker is present, your Swanphone will flash green.'

'But there might be hundreds of computers in

Korolev's castle,' says Spencer. 'We won't have time to check them all.'

'Alas, it is the only way. If you're not thorough, the Nutcracker could slip through the net. Korolev will have won, and mankind will have lost.'

'Any other questions?' asks the Captain.

I look around at the pale faces. No one puts their hands up. The Nutcracker seems to have sucked the air out of the room. 'In that case, I think we've kept Mr Kinsmeet for long enough. Thank you for coming out in this weather. I'll see you to your car.'

'It was my pleasure, Captain. I hope I've been of some help. Actually, would you mind if Milly wheeled me outside? She's an excellent driver.'

We whizz into the empty lobby. I loop the loop around Dame Anna Popova, zoom into the porch and pull up sharply. The slope running alongside the stairs is black with ice and sleet is splattering the gravel. I tuck Mr Kinsmeet's blanket around his shoulders.

'Thank you, Milly. Would you send my best wishes to your mother? I was so pleased to hear of her rescue last year. Such a wonderful lady.'

'Thanks. I'll tell her when I see her. She was supposed to be here today but—'

My eyes begin to prickle and before I can stop them, tears are streaming down my cheeks. 'I'm s-so sorry, Mr Kinsmeet. I don't know what's c-come over me.'

'Milly, my dear, don't mind me. I imagine your mother is away, which must be a constant worry for you. The Mouse King is a tricky customer and your friends are about to undertake a very dangerous mission. At Swan House, we place so much responsibility on young shoulders. I confess, I'm surprised Ms Celia is placing so much faith in a showman like Max Deverall. When he was in school, I suspected his bravado only went skin deep.'

I swipe the tears and sleet from my eyes. 'You taught Max when he was here, didn't you, Mr Kinsmeet?'

Mr Kinsmeet folds his speckly old hands on his lap. 'I did. Why do you ask?'

Without thinking, I blurt out the whole story. I tell him what Mr Stubbs said about jokers and spots, about Max's mysterious phone call, about his secret rendezvous in the tunnels.

'. . . But none of the teachers believe me. And now the Deveralls are leading the mission when they could be working with Korolev, or worse. He could be the actual Mouse King . . .' I gulp down another sob. 'And I won't be there to stop him. Mr Kinsmeet, what should I do?'

Mr Kinsmeet brings his face closer to mine. His

voice tiptoes into my ears. 'Are you sure, Milly? Do you have evidence?'

I shake my head and he pats my hand.

'Then my dear, you must find some. It is imperative that Swan House goes to Casova and destroys the Nutcracker. The Deveralls cannot be allowed to get in the way.'

22

The Deeply Suspicious Sou'wester

When we get back to the dorm that night, there are brown-paper packages labelled *Operation Nutcracker* on two of the beds. The only thing on mine is a cold hot-water bottle cat.

Leonora shakes out a mottled grey leotard, complete with hood and a pair of goggles. 'It's my Swansuit,' she says, turning the label over. 'Madge says the thermal fabric is waterproof, tearproof and bulletproof.'

'Cor,' says Lottie. 'Feels like a wetsuit.'

They wriggle into their Swansuits while I pull on my pyjamas.

Lottie tries on the goggles. 'Cool. They're night-vision goggles. I'm like you now, Leo.'

'In what way?' asks Leonora.

'Half flippin' owl!'

Leonora's face is blank. 'I don't know what you mean.'

I catch Lottie's eye before it flicks to her Swan-phone. 'It's a message from the Captain. Come on, we got one last trainin' session.'

'But it's dark,' I say. 'Why can't it wait until the morning now the inspector's gone?'

''Cos the mission's at night, ain't it? We need to train in the same conditions.'

'It's OK, Milly,' says Leonora. 'You don't need to worry about the dark. This session is just for us. Where is it, Lottie?'

I grind my teeth.

'Outside,' says Lottie with a grimace. 'Max and the Captain are waitin' at the Dance of Death.'

Leonora tells me to stay behind. I tell her that she's not Ms Celia and she can keep her orders to herself, but I do as I'm told and give Lottie a tight little smile as she leaves.

The second they've gone, I put on my hoody, pop my drone into my utility belt and fasten it around my waist.

Evidence, I need evidence.

The courtyard is clear. I follow the voices crossing the field and head towards the boundary. Taking cover behind a tree, I hold my breath as Max says, 'Everyone's present, Captain.'

Peering from behind the tree trunk, I spot a stretcher lying on the grass next to the fence. Nurse sets her first aid kit next to it and adjusts her cap. A little further along, Jada nudges William Fynn. He shifts nervously from foot to foot.

The Captain steps into the moonlight. 'Listen carefully. When we reach the castle, our first challenge is to climb the eastern rampart. Unlike the ramparts to the north, south and west, it has no walkway behind it. This means in order to reach the towers, we'll have to jump along the crenellated parapet at the top.'

He points up at the fence posts.

'The good news is the crenels are similarly spaced to the posts in our own Dance of Death – a *grand jeté* apart. The bad news is that's where you'll be training tonight. So, who wants to go first?'

Lottie, Leonora, Bumble and Spencer put their hands up. They must be totally off their ramparts.

'Let Leo go first,' says Max. 'She's done a lot worse.'

Leonora scales the fence like a cat. She balances on the top of the first post, before jumping lightly to the second. She makes it look easy. After three more jumps, Max helps her down. He gives her a high five.

'Well done, pet,' says the Captain. 'That was pure textbook. OK, Li, your turn.'

I cross my fingers as Lottie hugs the post and starts to shimmy up.

She *jetés* from the first to the second post. On the third a gust of wind blows her off balance. She tilts one way, then the other.

'You can do it, Shorty!' shouts Spencer.

I suck in my breath.

Somehow, Lottie manages to straighten up and carry on. I don't breathe again until she's back on the ground.

Spencer's just as brave. He flies around, earning a reluctant 'Well done' from Max.

It's Bumble next. She doesn't have Leonora's grace, Lottie's strength or Spencer's long legs, but she does have a kind of recklessness that makes me want to vomit.

'Take it a bit slower in Casova, OK?' says the Captain as he helps her down. 'OK, who's next?'

Will blinks. 'Ladies first,' he says to Jada.

Oh dear. Was that the Blink of Fear? I can hear it in his voice, see it in his knees. Jada's never failed a test in her life and has no intention of starting now. But when Will starts to jump, I look away just in time. The thud as he hits the ground makes my bones crunch.

There's silence as Max and Nurse rush him to the infirmary. I lean against the tree shaking. A tiny twig snaps under my foot and before I know it, I'm pinned against the trunk with my arms behind my back and something cold and metallic in my face.

'Hen's teeth, Kydd!' The Captain lowers the hair-spray doobrie in his hand. 'I could have hurt you. What the blazes do you think you're doing?'

He heaves me back to my feet and I watch his expression change from anger to irritation.

'Spit it out.'

'I want to do it.' *Who said that?* 'I saw Will fall just now and everyone else has been sent home. You need eight people to go to Casova. I want to go. I want to do the Dance of Death.' *Who is that lunatic talking?*

Both of the Captain's ponytails swing in disbelief. 'You're volunteering to do the Dance of Death?'

'Yes.'

'You understand even if you survive, there's no guarantee that Max will agree to take you?'

'Yes, but he might.' I glance at Leonora, whose spy-face is trying very hard not to argue.

Spencer steps up. 'Let her prove she can do it. If she can't, you don't take her. What have you got to lose?'

After a pause, the Captain shrugs. 'OK, but for the record, it's against my better judgement.'

Climbing up should be the easy bit but it's harder than it looks. By the time I've reached the top, my fingers are full of splinters and my head is full of doubt. I don't want to move and I especially don't want to jump, but the wind's got other ideas. It moans and the post shifts under my feet. My arms fly into second postion – half ballet dancer, half tightrope walker. I make a moany-windy noise myself.

'What are you waiting for?' shouts the Captain. 'Stop bliddy star gazing and get on with it!'

The next post seems miles away, but I have to get to Casova. I have to stop Max and Leonora. I have to save the world!

One small jeté for woman – one giant jeté for womankind.

I say a prayer to the Viking gods, and jump.

As the soles of my feet pound the fence, every *jeté*, every landing, every breath feels like a victory over the Deveralls.

'Go, Milly!' cheers Lottie.

The last post is in sight and her shout soars me into the air. Too high. I come down hard and something slides down my leg. I hold my balance and glance down. My belt is undone and my doobries have tumbled to the mud.

Bumble and Spencer run over and help me to the ground. 'Well done, Milky Bar.'

Lottie punches me on the arm. 'That took pluck. Told you she was brave, Leo.'

214

Leonora gives me a watery smile.

'Well done, pet,' says the Captain. 'You never fail to surprise us.'

His grin fades as Max tramps across the frozen mud. 'What was she doing up there? Isn't one trip to the infirmary enough for one night?'

'But she did it without falling,' says Jada, giving me a grudging nod. 'How's Will?'

'He's got concussion and a broken nose. He's going to be out of action for a while.'

'So does that mean I can go, Captain?' I say.

'Go where?' asks Max.

'To Casova.'

'Who said you could go to Casova?' says Max. 'Captain, we talked about this, I made a promise.'

A promise? A promise to who? I fold my arms. 'You just said it yourself, Will's going to be out of action for ages!'

'I said no, Milly.'

My heart sinks into the mud.

'But we're a man down, Max,' says the Captain.

Max glances at his Swanphone and takes the Captain aside. 'Listen, I've got to pick up a few things from Eva's before we leave. We'll talk about this when I get back.'

I don't hear the Captain's response. Jada starts herding us towards the school. 'I'll catch you up,' I say, pointing at the the scattered contents of my utility belt.

I scoop up the rosin, the lip salve, the hairspray, the pins. But the drone's not here. It can't have gone far. I sweep the light of my Swanphone along the foot of the fence.

Where is it?

I get on my hands on knees. Peer under leaves. Burrow into nettles. Dig the icy mud until my hands are numb.

When my Swanphone starts to flash, I realize I've completely lost track of time.

'Alert. The temperature has dropped to minus one degree celsius. You are strongly advised to add a thick thermal layer to your current attire or go indoors.'

The drone must have rolled further into the woods. I'll have to come back in the morning. Taking a last look at the treeline, I stop dead.

A dark shape is following the fence. A man. He looks over his shoulder in a deeply suspicious manner and the moon lights up his face.

My heart thuds. I know that face.

He pulls his collar up over his ears and slinks into the dense, dark woods.

Fastening my utility belt, I slink into the dense, dark woods after him.

Trying to remember everything the Captain taught us about evasion and tracking, I keep well back and make myself as trunk-like as possible. My target darts between the trees and melts into the shadows. He reappears and glances over his shoulder. Me and my PJs have no choice but to throw ourselves into an icy puddle.

Luckily he doesn't seem to notice the splash. He pauses where the path forks three ways and pulls on a pair of Madge's night-vision goggles. My target moves further into the woods, towards the lake. The holly and ivy knit together, as thick as a Christmas tank top. It's like all the dark in the world has met for a convention.

Footsteps squelch into the fog. The man turns into a ghost. He whistles a ghostly tune.

My ears twitch. I know that tune.

He stops whistling and starts to whisper. Not in English. Not in French or Russian. In Casovan.

'Over here!'

I know that voice.

I separate the branches. There's a sound like oars slapping the water, and a small boat breaks through the fog. The boat rocks as the rower stands up. I can't see a face but he's wearing a sou'wester and galoshes, like the Bombardier on one of his a fly-fishing weekends.

The boat noses the bank. It sways as my target steps inside.

'You came,' says Max Deverall.

Hugo's words whisper in my ear. *Do you have evidence?*

I hold up my Swanphone and begin to film.

23

Stepping into Supergirl's Shoes

As the boat recedes into the fog, there's a snap behind me. I whimper before a hand clamps over my mouth.

'Shhh,' says a voice. The hand falls away and I spin around.

'Lottie? What are you doing here?'

'The Captain sent me back for you. I saw you sneakin' off and followed. You ain't that brilliant at evasion and trackin' you know. Anyway, who was that in the boat?'

I hesitate. Should I tell Lottie what I just saw or go straight to the Captain?

'Well?' says Lottie.

I want her to believe me more than anyone, and she did say I was brave. 'It was Max Deverall,' I say.

Lottie stamps her foot. 'You never learn, do you?'

'I took pictures, Lottie. Look.'

Lottie stares at my Swanphone. Her hand flies to her mouth.

'I don't flamin' believe it. Do you know who was wiv him?'

'I couldn't see. They were wearing a sou'wester.'

'A sour what? Aw, never mind, let me see that again.'

I rerun the video. 'They're talking in Casovan.'

'Can you make it louder? I can't hear.'

'Sorry, it's on full volume. Once Max climbed in the boat, I couldn't hear what they were saying.'

'What's he playin' at?'

Lottie chomps on her nails as I repeat everything I told Mr Kinsmeet.

'Sorry, Milly, I feel like a right banana. I fought you was sayin' all that stuff about the Deveralls cos you was jealous. I should've listened to you from the start.'

I bow my head. 'I'm sorry too. I *was* jealous. I thought Leonora was going to take you away from me like Max had taken Mum. I was looking for reasons not to trust them, but then Max started behaving weirdly and I realized he really was up to something.'

'So what do we do now?'

She said *we*. Lottie believes me and she's going to help. Suddenly I feel lighter than the Sugar Plum

Fairy. 'We've got to tell the Captain before Max gets back.'

Lottie holds out her hand. We start to shake then, with a whoosh of happiness, we throw our arms around each other.

The Captain is waiting for us in the courtyard. His beard is sideways with tugging. 'Where've you two been?'

I watch Leonora disappear inside the coach house.

'Show him, Milly,' says Lottie.

'Show me what?'

'It's about Max,' I say.

The Captain glances at the coach house door. 'You'd better come with us.'

Lottie and I follow him into a dark and empty refectory. With no children to feed, Cook's taken Topsy to Brighton to get some sea air. The Captain doesn't bother to turn on the lights.

'Well?'

'Captain, when I was picking up my doobries, I saw Max out in the woods. He was doing this . . .' I look over my shoulder in a deeply suspicious manner. 'So I followed him to the lake.'

The refectory is so echoey, it sounds like I'm telling tales on myself.

'To the *lake*?'

'Yes. He met someone on a boat – I couldn't see their face—'

'He was wearin' a sour wester,' adds Lottie.

'A what?'

'Never mind. Captain, Max is in cahoots with Ivan Korolev. I think he might even be the Mouse King.'

The Captain cracks his enormous knuckles. My ears cringe.

'Where's your evidence? That's a very serious accusation.'

'Milly filmed them,' says Lottie. 'They were talking in Casovan.'

I play back the video on my Swanphone. When Max climbs into the boat, the Captain begins to rumble. When I tell him everything I told Mr Kinsmeet, he starts to shake.

'Wait here.'

Lottie and I watch him march into the corridor and speak into his Swanphone.

'Who do you fink he's callin'?' says Lottie.

'I don't know. Could be Ms Celia? Mum's still out of reach.'

Lottie digs me in the ribs as the door on to the courtyard opens. Leonora peers inside. 'I thought I heard voices – have you seen Dad? The lab's come back with the test results on the umbrella. As well as gunpowder, there were very faint traces of rosin.'

I shoot a look at Lottie. That proves that Max and Leonora had something to do with the fireworks in the Opera House.

Leonora takes in our expressions. Lottie's, accusing. Mine, triumphant. I avoid the question mark in her eyes.

'I fought he'd gone to Clapham,' says Lottie.

'He did,' she replies. 'But he said he'd be back by now.'

I stare at her face, but there isn't a flicker of guilt. She should join Willow Perkins in Hollywood.

There are footsteps on the cobbles behind her, and Leonora smiles. 'Oh, it's OK, he's here. Dad, you've been ages. I thou—'

Coat-tails flying, Max pushes past her into the refectory. His cheeks are flushed and his curls are stuck to his forehead. 'Sorry Leo, couldn't find what I was looking for. Is the Captain here?'

Lottie points at the corridor and Leonora follows Max across the refectory.

I check his shoes – clean as a whistle. You've got to give it to him – he's a brilliant spy, but you can't wipe the outdoors off your cheeks.

There's a rumble from the corridor, and before you can say 'suspicious sou'wester', the Captain is face to face with the Deveralls. 'Maximillian Deverall,' he says. 'Pending investigation, I'm suspending you from duty with immediate effect.'

For a second, Leonora's spy-face vanishes. For a second, it's like I'm seeing her real face for the first time. Not an angry or wicked face – a sad face I can't bear to look at.

Max laughs. 'What am I supposed to have done?'

'It's alleged that you've broken the Swan House Code of Conduct.'

The laughter stops. 'Wait a minute, has this got anything to do with her?' He points at me.

'That's irrelevant,' says the Captain.

Leonora says to Lottie. 'You don't believe Dad's done anything wrong, do you, Lottie?'

Lottie juts out her dimply chin. 'Rule Firty-free of *The Guide to Espionage*. If somefink looks like a snake and hisses like a snake, you can bet your flamin' tutu it bites like a snake.'

Max's hand shoots to his wrist.

'I think you'll find that your Swanphones have been disabled.' The Captain aims his Swanphone at Max. 'Please don't try anything stupid.'

A dot of red light dances on Max's jacket. Sugar Plum Fairies! It's the Captain's zipper.

Max smiles and drops his hands to his sides. 'Don't be a fool, Garth. What about the mission? You *need* us!'

The Captain's shadow looms over Max. 'Neither of you are going anywhere until we've got to the bottom of this. Li, you come with us. We'll take them to the gym until I get further instructions.'

He pauses at the door. 'And Kydd, you'd better get ready. You're going to Casova.'

I head back to the dorm. Lottie believes me. The Captain believes me. I got what I wanted. So why do I feel so miserable?

Maybe it was the look on Leonora's face?

Doubt wriggles inside me. But what about the evidence? The fireworks at *The Nutcracker*, Max's disappearance from Meekes, the doll in my house, the secret rendezvous, the man in the suspicious sou'wester? That was no fishing trip – the Deveralls are guilty, what other explanation could there be?

I summon the only person I know who always looks on the bright side.

'Greetings, Milly. What can I— Oh, dear, what is it? Are you upset? It isn't my fault, is it? I seem to keep getting things wrong. My wires are all crossed.'

'No, it's not you, Trevor. It's me. I told on the Deveralls and now I feel miserable and I don't know why.'

'Max and Leonora? What did they do?'

'I think Max is the Mouse King.'

Trevor's beam wobbles. 'Max Deverall – the Mouse King? Oh no, I don't think that can be right. Wait a minute. Just uncrossing some wires. It's on the tip of my tongue . . .'

'No, Trevor, people have been telling me I'm wrong since I got here, but I'm right, I know I am.'

'Rule Thirteen,' says Trevor. 'That's right – Rule Thirteen: The things you seek are often right under your nose.'

'What? No, listen, I don't know his plan, but Max has got something to do with Korolev and the Nutcracker.'

'The Nu-*uh-oh*.' Trevor pops into thin air.

I decide to never switch on my mentor again.

Pushing Trevor out of my mind, I start to get ready for the mission. I don't have a Swansuit so I lay out my tracksuit and trainers. I put the utility belt with Madge's doobries on top. Last of all, I take Mum's bracelet from my music box and lay it on the pile. Looking at it, I feel another wriggle of doubt. What's Mum going to say about the Deveralls? Will she be sad about Max? Will she be angry with me?

All the next day, even with Lottie being nice, and Jada being sorry, and the Captain giving us lots to do, I can't shake off the feeling that I've done something wrong.

My last job before we go is to collect our updated Swanphones from Merv. I haven't seen him since Max and Leonora were suspended and brace myself for the inevitable hrumphing.

Merv is crouched between monitors and sandwich boxes reading *The Tools of the Trade*.

'Hi Merv.'

'Oh, it's you. Your Swanphones are on the desk.' He gestures at a box without looking up. 'Remember, you have to turn on the Nutcracker sensor or it won't work.'

I pick up the box and wait for him to wish me luck, but he doesn't.

'Is that it? I'm about to go on a deadly, dangerous mission. I might not come back, you know.'

Merv swivels his chair. 'If our intelligence is correct and most of Korolev's students are at the president's palace, there is a 73.5 per cent chance that you'll be back this time tomorrow.'

'Is 73.5 per cent good?'

Merv hrumphs. 'The odds would have been a lot better if you were taking the Deveralls.' He shakes his head. 'Either way, me wishing you luck isn't going to change anything.'

I hrumph back at him. 'Where are they now? The Deveralls, I mean.'

Merv sniffs. 'Can't say.'

'Just tell me if they're still in the school.'

Merv sighs. 'They're on their way to a secure facility. For some reason, the Captain didn't trust me to watch over them while you were gone.'

A secure facility? Oh dear. That doesn't sound like somewhere you can dance. I squish down the guilt. I suppose I should have thought of that before I dobbed them in.

'Bye then, Merv. If I don't see you again, go forth and prosper and all that.'

Eyes back on his book, Merv does a Mr Spock thing with his fingers.

I think I see the tiniest smile.

Waiting for me on the bed when I get back to the dorm is a small brown package labelled *Operation Nutcracker*.

'From Madge,' says Lottie with a dimply grin. 'Let's get changed.'

As the sun sinks low and the sky turns blood red, we pull on Madge's Swansuits and clip on our belts. I tuck my bracelet with its boomerbang charm into my sleeve.

There's a knock on the door. 'You ready, girls?' says Jada Gayle. She looks like Catgirl.

'You bet!' says Lottie.

'The Captain says to wear your climbing harnesses under your belts and be quick about it. He's tearing out his beard.'

'What's wrong now?' says Lottie, wriggling into her harness.

Jada sighs. 'The Deveralls have denied everything and are refusing to talk. Who knows what we'll come up against in Casova . . . Milly, this isn't a sleepover. You can leave the hot-water bottle behind.'

I lay Boris on my bed with a huff and clip on my harness. I wish I had the drone but it's still in the woods.

We step into the night air and make our way silently to the coach house. Parked next to Winifred is Earnest, a sweet little red Reliant Robin who's been transformed into Winifred's superjet sidekick.

Bumble is perched on one of Earnest's wings, randomly freezing and defrosting her own fingers with her Swanphone. 'This is fun,' she says.

Spencer has snuck into Earnest's cockpit.

'Hey, Spencer, get out of there before the Captain sees you,' says Jada. 'And no more messing about. Without the two strongest members of the team, we all need to step up.' She shoos Bumble off the wing then frowns at me. 'Especially you, Milly. You're stepping into some very big shoes.'

I swallow hard. She means Leonora. I'm stepping into Supergirl's shoes.

The Captain's voice booms across the courtyard. 'It's 2200 hours. Is everyone here?'

He emerges from the coach house and Lottie's mouth drops open. In his Swansuit, the Captain is as sleek and predatory as a great white shark.

'Kydd and Bee, you're in Winifred with me. Spencer and Li, you're in Earnest with Gayle. Well, don't just stand there. Get in!'

Spencer waits for Lottie to climb in the back and grins at Jada. 'Are you sure you want to drive?'

Jada scowls. 'Shut up and get in with Li.' She slams the cockpit door.

Bumble and I squeeze into Winifred. The Captain hunches up in the front. Even convertible Morris Minors aren't big enough for Viking gods.

'Belts on, and make sure they stay on,' he says.

He presses a button and pulls a lever. There's enough roaring to make my teeth rattle and next thing I know, we're high above the school. Then with a jolt that almost dislocates my eyeballs, we're off.

24

Operation Nutcracker

For the first twenty minutes, we climb almost vertically. My heart is in my mouth. It's like all my organs have swapped places.

As we rise above the swirling clouds, Bumble files her nails, totally unbothered. 'Wonder what Leonora's doing now,' she says. I frown as she smiles her upside-down smile. 'Everyone was wrong except us, weren't they, Milly? I bet we'll get a hero's welcome when we get back. They'll all want to hang out with us.'

From the front seat, there's a rumble that isn't Winifred. 'Quiet, Bee. Our ETA is 0200 hours. I'd get some sleep if I were you.'

If I crick my neck and rub a little hole in the condensation, I can just see out of Winifred's window. I squash down thoughts of Leonora and what's waiting for us in Casova and gaze out into the starless sky.

'Wake up, you two. We're starting our descent,' says the Captain. 'Fifteen minutes until we reach our destination.'

Bumble yawns and looks out of the window. We're sinking lower and lower and so is my stomach.

'I didn't expect Casova to be so pretty. Did you see the forests in the moonlight – and all the snow and frozen lakes? It was like a fairy tale from one of those old picture books my babushka used to—'

'Give it a rest, Kydd,' says the Captain.

I know I'm talking rubbish but I can't seem to stop. 'I read they've got all kinds of wild animals here too – boars, bears, tigers, wolves – did I say bears?'

White-tipped mountains give way to an angry, black sea. Three jagged rocks loom out of the mist like a grim welcoming committee. Towering behind them are sheer, black cliffs.

'Look,' says Bumble. 'Right at the top.'

Framed by a blood-red moon squats Korolev's castle. Bathed in mist, it clings like a seabird to the edge of the outcrop. Below is a sheer drop to the waves.

'Black Lodge,' says the Captain.

I try not to whimper. 'How are we going to land?'

Bumble says, 'Winifred's built for impossible landings – you'll see.'

There's a thunk from Winifred's undercarriage.

'Wheels deployed for landing,' says the Captain. 'Hold on back there.'

Bumble laughs as the world turns upside down. For the longest moment, we seem to hang motionless, then there's a jolt and the engine dies. I force myself to look out of the window. Where did the sky go? Everything's in the wrong place – we're hanging on to the cliff like a bat.

'How is Winifred doing that?'

'Suction-cup tyres,' says the Captain.

Bumble reaches for the door. 'Can we go now?'

'Not before you've clipped your gear to your harnesses. And use some of this.' He passes us a little pouch. 'It's chalk – like rosin for your hands.'

The Captain fastens a bandolier across his body and throws open his door. The weather roars and spits its way inside. Still holding on to Winifred, he glances up at the castle. His ponytail whips the window as he lets go and grabs the rock.

Bumble and I clamber out next to him and huddle under Winifred's wing. The cold cuts through my Swansuit and three layers of thermal underwear. I make sure my bracelet is still tucked safely in my sleeve.

'Don't look down,' shouts the Captain.

Too late. We're so high up, one little slip would be terminal.

I thread the rope through my harness with trembly fingers. The mineral smell of wet cliff goes up my nose.

The Captain issues instructions. 'Bee, wait here until I reach the top. Kydd, you follow Bee. As long as you both remember your training, no one will get hurrrrr . . .'

His words splinter into the sky. The Captain finds a foothold and grips the craggy rock with a craggy hand. Steadily, he moves upwards and sideways into the mist, only pausing to anchor the rope to the cliff while we take in the slack. He's right; climbing is like a slow, vertical dance. Upwards and sideways, upwards and sideways, until at last he heaves himself over the ledge.

The Captain is a rock-climbing god.

I crane my neck as he shouts down. 'Your turn, Bee. Take it slowly!'

'Break a leg, Bumble.' The spray is salty on my tongue.

She laughs grimly. 'You too.'

Bumble climbs like a little grey tarantula, fearless and quick. In no time at all, the Captain's pulling her over the ledge.

My turn. I rub together my clammy hands and wish I had more chalk.

The Captain's shout swoops down from the ledge. 'Come on, Kydd. We've got you.'

I channel my inner tarantula and grip the icy rock. Blanking out the boom of the waves below, I use my legs to push up and start to feel a rhythm. The clippy-things the Captain calls quickdraws clink a noisy tune against my leg.

'Nearly there,' he shouts.

I look up. Gnarly fingers reach through the mist towards me. I stretch out my hand, but there's a roar from above. A dark shape is plummeting towards us.

'Kydd!' yells the Captain as I tumble backwards. My stomach lurches. I bash against the rock and come to a dangling stop as Earnest settles on the cliff.

'Hang on!' shouts the Captain.

'I'm trying!'

I grip the rope so tightly my fingers bleed. Finally, he heaves me over the edge. Next to Winifred, Earnest's door opens and out slides Jada.

The adventure has only just begun.

Scaling the ramparts is almost as hard as climbing the cliff. Black Lodge is carved from slabs as black and slippery as the rock itself. Once we're crouched at the top of the parapet, the Captain secures ropes ready for our escape.

'So far so good,' he says. 'Max fed the correct coordinates into the convertibles, but without Leonora, we can't disable the security system. So, Li, you're with me – we'll head east to the Watch Tower and immobilize the lookouts before searching the Prison Tower. Gayle and Bee, you make your way to the Weapons Tower. Spencer and Kydd, you go west to the Dance Tower. If you find a suspect device, use your sensor. If it turns green, call me immediately. Right, do you all know what to do?'

Everyone nods.

'One last thing,' says the Captain, 'if something goes wrong, action a Code Pink. We'll meet back here at 0630 hours Juliet. Don't be late – the sun rises at 0728.'

I whisper to Spencer. 'What's *Romeo and Juliet* got to do with this?'

'*Juliet* means *local time* – haven't you learnt anything in Spy Craft?'

When I look blank, Spencer says, 'Leave everything to me, especially the bad guys.'

'Bad guys? But I thought everyone was in the president's palace? And didn't the Captain say he was going to deal with the lookouts?'

Spencer takes my shoulders. 'Let's worry about one thing at a time. Ready to *jeté* across the crenels?'

I nod silently. Disappearing into the mist, the stone parapet makes the Dance of Death look like the hokey-cokey.

'Break a leg, Milky Bar,' says Spencer in an un-Spencerly solemn tone. 'And please try not to do anything stupid.'

The mist lifts as Spencer starts to leap along the parapet. I watch *jeté* after *grand jeté* – it's like he's flying across the moon.

I teeter on the edge, sea mist seeping through my suit and into my confidence. '*You can't do that. You'll fall,*' says a little voice burrowing into my head. '*Leave it to Spencer and Bumble. They'll find the Nutcracker, won't they?*'

Spencer calls out. 'Come on, Kyyyyyydd! What are you waiting forrrrrr?'

I rub salty tears from my eyes. 'I can't do it, Spencer,' but my words are drowned by the waves. I lift my Swanphone to call him, but it's already flashing.

It's a message.

Milly, there's so much to say, but for now I want you to know I have faith in you. I'm so proud of you, sweetheart. Do what has to be done, then come home safe. Love Mum x

A gust of wind pushes me back, but I hold strong. Heart singing, I howl like the wind and start to fly.

'For just a second there, I thought you weren't going to do it,' says Spencer, hauling me to safety.

I cling to the rough stone and grin. 'S'pose all I have to do now is not do anything stupid.'

'Too late.' Spencer points at my utility belt.

I tug the zip. 'Uh-oh, it's broken again. All my doobries have fallen out.'

'At least you've still got your Swanphone,' he says, aiming his wrist at the tower door. 'Stand back.'

With a lightning flash and a bang silenced by the waves, the door falls open.

Clambering over the debris, we find ourselves on a narrow stone staircase – one of those winding ones that goes on for ever and makes you feel dizzy by the time you reach the bottom. Right opposite us is a heavy oak door.

'If Max's hologram castle was accurate, there are three floors in the tower,' whispers Spencer. 'Two dance studios and a wardrobe department at the top. Guess this is the entrance.'

I reach for the door's frozen handle. 'May as well start here and work our way down.'

'Good plan. Let's go.'

The door creaks open and we peer inside. There's a cold, damp graveyard feel to the place and it's so dark I can't see my own feet. I order my Swanphone to light the way, but nothing happens.

'Uh-oh.'

'What is it now?'

'My Swanphone's gone dead.'

'What have you done to it?'

'Nothing, it was fine a moment ago. Try yours.'

'For Crump's sake!' says Spencer, forgetting to whisper. 'Mine's not working either. Well, there's nothing we can do about it now. Put on your goggles and stay close.'

I fiddle around with Madge's night-vision goggles and suddenly everything has an eerie green glow.

'This is properly cool,' says Spencer, looking like a teenage Incredible Hulk with nicer hair. He holds up a green hand and gestures to the left.

Eyes wide, I take in the weird green shapes – tables, clothes rails, a mannequin . . . 'I'll start with the table, then the chest of drawers, and then—'

'Shhh, Milky Bar, I don't need the running commentary.'

My fingers run over a large staple gun and a sewing box brimming with needles and pins – all potential weapons if you were as ruthless as Ivan Korolev.

'Do you think the Captain's taken care of the lookouts yet?' I ask Spencer, hoping with every fibre of my being that I won't be forced to defend myself with a staple gun and crimping scissors.

My foot hits something under the table.

'Ooo, Spencer, I think I've found some kind of case.' I lift it on to the table and the staple gun falls with a thud.

'Keep the noise down, Kydd.'

'Blimey, Spence. It's really heavy. There might be a computer in— Uh-oh.'

'What is it *this* time?'

'Did you hear that?'

There's a whoosh behind me. 'The mannequin!' yells Spencer. 'BAD GUY!'

A foot whizzes past my ear. I duck a fist, dodge an elbow, slide across the table, swing from the curtain, land on a chair. Lean backwards, bend forwards, karate kick (woohoo – the Captain would be super-impressed). Then I lose my balance, and fall with an *oomph* right on top of the bad guy.

Spencer throws himself on both of us. Somehow I manage to wriggle free and crawl towards the table. There's a whirl of knuckles and legs and Spencer cries *'Aiyaah!'*

The bad guy's bare feet appear centimetres from my face. I stick out a foot and he topples over, hitting his head with a *thunk*. I scramble to my feet and, in total desperation, fashion a gag out of paper, then fasten it together with the staple gun. I think one of the staples goes through his ear. Sorry, bad guy.

Spencer is back on his feet. 'Where's that case?' he pants.

I lean on the table and open it shakily.

'Well?'

'Not it. Unless it's a sewing machine in disguise.'

'Doubt it.' He shakes his wrist. 'And we can't use the sensor until my Swanphone reboots.'

The bad guy starts to stir and I kneel over him. 'Have you found the Nutcracker? Tell us where it is, or . . . or . . . *or else*!'

I think he's cursing in Casovan, but it's hard to tell with his face wrapped in origami.

'I'll take care of him,' says Spencer. 'You carry on with the search.'

Tucking the staple gun into my harness, I head back to the staircase and rush down and down and round and round until I reach the floor below. I creep into the studio but apart from the barres lining the walls it's empty. Wiping the sweat from my eyes, I wonder if the bad guy's talking. Either way, I wish Spencer would hurry up.

Hand on the staple gun, I *tip-tap* down to the ground-floor studio. The noise of a door rattling in the wind and an ice-cold draught rises up the stairs to greet me.

Panting, I hesitate at the bottom of the stairwell. There are two doors. The nearest must lead to a walkway outside. Praying I don't bump into any more bad guys, I take a breath and let myself into the studio.

My eyes run along the barres and mirrors. They rest on a tall, dark cupboard in the corner – the perfect place to hide a computer. As I rush towards it, I trip over a bottle of water lying on the floor. Next to it is a crumpled sweatshirt and a half-eaten banana. Looks like someone's been rehearsing here tonight and if the banana is anything to go by, they're planning to come back at any min— a slam from outside makes my heart thud.

It came from the other door.

Don't panic, Milly. It could have been the wind.

I reach for the cupboard and freeze.

The wind doesn't have feet that *tip-tap* on stone floors. Or a voice that mutters to itself. Or fingers that can turn cast iron handles . . .

I try the cupboard door, but it's locked.

Tip-tap. Tip-tap.

There's nowhere to hide. All I can do is press myself into an alcove and will myself invisible.

A figure appears in the doorway. A girl – weirdly green and yet strangely familiar.

At that same moment the moonlight slips through

the windows and lights me up like a small, trembly Christmas tree.

A ghoulish green smile plays on the girl's lips and my stomach twists.

'Vell, vell, vell. Millicent Kydd. I vas hoping ve'd meet again.'

It's Korolev's star pupil, my old friend, Kristina the Knife. And true to her name, she's gripping something sharp and shiny.

25

Rule Thirteen

Kristina's eyes are green slits in the dark.

'Hello, Kristina,' I say in my jolliest voice. 'I was just looking for you.'

Kristina circles me like a wolf with pretty blonde braids. 'Vell, you've found me. Vhat are you doing here, Millicent?'

'I've, um, defected – turned to the dark side and all that.' I pull the meanest face I can muster. 'See?'

Kristina's pointy green knife twists in her hand. 'That vas pathetic. Tell me the truth, or I vill cut out your tongue and feed it to the gulls.'

'Well, it's nice to see you too,' I say, not taking my eyes from the knife. 'Actually, I've come for the Nutcracker. You don't know where it is, do you?'

'The Nutcracker?' Kristina's face breaks into a smirk. 'You mean the elusive veapon? Ha! Has the Mouse King been playing games vith Svan House too? I'm afraid you have come all this vay for nothing. For days ve have been searching. Every corner of the castle has been turned upside down. The Nutcracker is not in Black Lodge.'

'What do you mean? It has to be here. You're lying . . .'

'Vhy should I lie? In less than a minute, you vill be dead.'

When I swipe the sweat from eyes, I notice the bump in my sleeve. My bracelet!

I laugh. 'That's what you think!'

Kristina laughs back. 'Come on then, English girl. Show me vhat you can do!'

In one swift move, Kristina throws her knife.

In a swifter move, I hold up the boomerbang charm and watch a very strange thing happen. The knife stops mid-air.

It flicks around.

It hurtles back at its owner.

Kristina screams and ducks. The knife pierces her braids and pins her to the door frame.

Praise the Viking gods!

'I'll just take that,' I say, stapling her braids to the open door and freeing the knife. Just to be on the safe side, I staple her clothes too.

Genius, even if I say so myself.

'You vill not get avay vith this!' chokes Kristina. 'You think because you stole our Scarlet Slipper and took our Head of Ballet, you can break into our castle—'

I stop mid-staple. 'Your Head of Ballet? We didn't take your Head of . . . Wait a minute, are you saying your Head of Ballet used to be *Max Deverall*?'

Kristina cackles. 'No, *hlúpe*. She was Juliet Sarova. Didn't you know? She is in love with Max Deverall. Eck – there is no accounting for taste.'

WHAT?

'Is Max in love with her too?'

'That is vhat I am telling you! Juliet ran away to be with Max veeks ago. It vas so romantic – NOT. Ivan vas, how do'you say in English . . . *livid*.'

The staple gun slips from my hands. Kristina must be lying, but then I remember that tune Max kept whistling – the one from *Romeo and Juliet*.

Gahhh. Suspicious phone calls. Secret rendezvous. Mysterious boatmen. Max wasn't betraying us – he was meeting his very own Juliet.

Nooo . . . I kick the staple gun. How could I have been so wrong? I don't *want* to be wrong! Max might be a liar and a show-off but he's not the Mouse King. All this time I've been blaming Max for everything and the only thing he's really guilty of is being in love, and not even with Mum! It's too tragic. Like *Romeo and Juliet* without the tutus.

Suddenly, Kristina's laughter is drowned by the

shriek of an alarm.

'Things are not going so vell for Svan House, after all,' she crows. 'Your stupid friends have set off the alarm. Vhen Ivan returns, he vill tear out your hearts and eat them for breakfast!'

I leave Kristina wriggling herself free, dash back up the narrow staircase and crash into Spencer mid-stair.

'We've got to get out of here!' he yells. 'The boy wouldn't talk. Did you find the Nutcracker?'

'It's not here.'

'How do you know?'

'Kristina the Knife told me. She said the Mouse King had lied to us both. And Spencer, there was something else—'

'Not here.' Spencer grabs my hand and drags me round and round and up and up until we're back on the parapet. Crouching against the icy wind, we listen to the *wah-wah-wah* of the alarm whirling across the sky.

'What did Kristina tell you?'

'Max Deverall isn't the Mouse King. He's not helping Korolev. He's not even a real bad guy.'

'What do you mean?'

'He's in love with Korolev's Head of Ballet. She'd run away to be with him and that's who he was meeting. She was the mysterious boatman.'

'It was all about a *girl*?' says Spencer in disbelief.

I nod miserably. 'This is all my fault, Spencer. If Leonora was here, she'd have disabled the alarm and Korolev wouldn't be on his way back from the president's palace. I've put everyone into even more danger. I'm officially the World's Worst Spy.'

'Second worst,' says Spencer. 'Topping's still number one.'

'But Trevor isn't that bad when you think about it,' I say. 'He helped Leonora crack the code and he . . . Sugar plum fairies – Spencer!'

'What?'

'Which rule did Trevor keep going on about?'

Spencer searches the sky. 'Milky Bar, I think we've got more important things to worry about than Trevor.'

'But what if Kristina was right when she said the Mouse King's just playing with us? What if this is a wild goose chase? What if the Mouse King's not trying to lead us *to* the Nutcracker, what if he's leading us *away*?' I flap my arms like Topsy. 'Spencer, look at me! Trevor isn't the World's Worst Spy at all – I think he was trying to tell me where the Nutcracker is!'

Spencer shakes his head like I've lost more than my doobries. 'Yeah, right. And where's that?'

'Swan House.'

'That's crazy. You were seriously wrong about the Deveralls. Why should I listen to you now?'

'You shouldn't. But we should all have listened to Trevor. He kept going on about Rule Thirteen. *Often the things you seek—*'

'*Are under your nose.* You think the Mouse King sent us away so he'd have the school to himself?'

I nod. 'Only he won't have the school to himself . . .'

We both shout. 'MERV!'

Spencer checks his Swanphone and curses. 'Still dead. We can't call him. We can't even tell the Captain.'

'And I just had a thought. If the Mouse King is already in the school, he could have turned off the Swanphones!'

Spencer straightens against the wind. 'We've got to leave right now.'

I grab his sleeve. 'But Korolev could arrive at any second. We can't just leave the others behind.'

'They'll be as keen to get out of here as we are. They might even be waiting in the convertibles now.'

'But how can we get back if they're not?'

Spencer grins. 'Earnest.'

Our dance across the parapet and abseil back down to Earnest is a terrifying blur, but we make it in one piece. Both convertibles are where we left them. There's no sign of the others. Spencer slides into Earnest's cockpit and I take one last look up at the cliff.

'Don't worry, Milky Bar, Lottie'll be fine. She's got the Captain, remember? Merv hasn't got anyone.'

I feel torn in two. 'I suppose you're right. Are you sure you know how to fly this thing?'

'Of course. I've read the manual, remember? Plus I can land a virtual Airbus A380 in a snowstorm. Watch and learn, Milky Bar. Watch and learn!'

I check my seatbelt. Spencer hits the ignition. Everything starts to shake. There's a *shlurp* and a shudder as the suction-cups release, then a sickening lurch as we drop.

Spencer scrabbles with the lever. 'Don't panic! All under control!'

Or at least, that's what I think he's saying. I can't hear him over my screams.

With a stomach-churning flip, Earnest rights himself, zooms away from the cliffs and we climb up into the storm-black clouds.

26

En Garde!

I don't let go of my seat until London is twinkling below us.

'You did it, Spencer!'

Spencer doesn't reply.

'What's the matter?'

'Did I mention Gayle confiscated the manual off me before I got to the part on landing?'

'You mean you don't know how to land?'

'Don't worry, Kydd. It's just a technicality. Seriously, how hard can it be?'

As it turns out, very.

I point out that Earnest is facing the wrong way, in case Spencer hadn't noticed.

'Earnest was programmed to land on a cliff,' he pants, pretending not to have lost control of the controls.

'Can't you *re*program him?'

'Do you think I hadn't thought of that? I'm trying to override the auto-setting.'

'I have no idea what that means, but can you please do it quickly!'

'I said I'm trying!'

'Try hard-*arghhhhhh . . .*'

Earnest's nose dips and we flip, rolling one way then the other, like a pair of socks in a tumble dryer. Swan House looms below us. Earnest clips a wing on the fence. He crashes through the trees. He *bump, bump, bumps* across the mud, wheels across the drive and spins to a whiplash stop on the lawn.

My fingers unfurl. I pat myself down. Open my eyes one at a time. My head is spinning but there's nothing broken.

'You OK?' I say to Spencer.

'Fine,' says Spencer. 'But my foot's stuck.'

I glance at Spencer's leg.

'Is it hurt?'

'I don't think so. Remember – we Spencers are like cats.'

'Well, I think you just lost one of your lives.'

'Don't worry, eight more left. It could take me a while to get out. Think you'll have to go without me. Don't worry, the Captain'll be here soon.'

As I wobble on to the ground, Spencer winds down his window.

'Good luck, Milky Bar. You did all right for a girl with a staple gun.'

I roll my eyes and turn towards the school. Darting from tree to tree, I make it to the steps, check over both shoulders and bound up to the front door.

And stop.

How am I going to get in without my Swanphone? But as I draw nearer I see the doors are wide open. Uh-oh. Anyone could swan right in.

The lobby is dark and silent. I jump when I see a figure, but it's only Dame Anna's statue. Quiet as a superspy, I pad up the stairs to the CR and open the door.

'Merv?'

The first thing I notice is the empty chair. The second thing I notice are the computers. The screens are blank. The cameras are off. Everything is down. No wonder our Swanphones aren't working.

I kick something and look down. It's Merv's thermos. It rolls over a slip of paper next to it.

A printout from Sid in the virtual library.

To Merv Crump.

Library overdue notice.

Book borrowed: The Tools of the Trade by Hugo Kinsmeet.

Underneath, Merv has written *hugo kinsmeet – huos kingmeet – house kingsmet*. Before I can figure out what that means, a flash of movement down in the theatre catches my eye. A long, brown cardigan and thick, tan tights disappear into the wings. Phew. It's only Miss Batty.

I tuck the printout in my sleeve, tear out of the control room, and gallop down the stairs to the theatre.

'Miss Batty! Have you seen Merv?'

Her cardigan whips around the corner. Her shoes clomp up the stairs.

'Miss Batty, wait! You could be in danger!'

I run up the staircase after her – all polished oak and brass stair rods. Why is she going to Lord Astus's suite? Won't it be locked now that Mr Brown has gone?

I pause at the top – the suite is vast. I look past a grand piano to the floor-to-ceiling windows, half hidden by swags of moth-eaten curtains. Shafts of dusty moonlight stripe a large, faded rug. The walls are hung with swords, shields and the Astus family's coat of arms. Overlooking a four-poster bed is a rusting suit of armour.

'Miss Batty,' I pant. 'Where are you?'

Curtains are drawn around the four-poster bed. Heart pounding, I creep towards it and tug them apart.

Metal clangs behind me. I spin around to find a sword pointing at my chest.

No.

This can't be happening.

Seriously?

'Miss Batty, it's me, Milly. What are you doing?'

Miss Batty lunges.

I fall back as everything I learnt from Max's fencing class goes out of my head.

Miss Batty slashes at the mattress. I roll across the bed – slide off the other side – reach for a sword on the wall.

Max said fencing was like a dance. I spin on my heels and spring forward. Miss Batty staggers back. She lunges again and I parry. Our blades clash and my wrist twists. She strikes again, but I *jeté* to one side, catch her off balance and with all my strength sweep her sword out of her hands. It clatters under the bed and Miss Batty drops to her knees.

'What have you done with Merv? He'd better be OK or . . . or . . .'

Her sweet face blinks up at me. 'I d-don't know what you're t-talking about.'

I point the tip of the sword at her arm and the printout falls from my sleeve.

It's the library notice.

Book borrowed: The Tools of the Trade by Hugo Kinsmeet.

The letters begin to dance in front of my eyes.

huos kinsmeet . . . house kingsmet . . . mouse kingeth . . . the mouse king.

THE MOUSE KING!

I stagger back, the sword trembling in my hand. Nice old Mr Kinsmeet is the Mouse King!

'You're lying, Miss Batty. The Mouse King is an anagram. You're helping Mr Kinsmeet, aren't you?'

'H-he needs me,' says Miss Batty.

'But he's evil!'

'You d-don't understand. How c-could you? You have family, friends, t-talent! I only had Swan House. I'd been here for five years when they decided I wasn't g-good enough. I was sixteen with nowhere to g-go. Mr Kinsmeet told me they needed a new p-piano player and when I said I c-couldn't play, he offered me a deal. If I would be his feet, he would b-be my hands.'

I lower the sword. 'I don't understand.'

'Mr Kinsmeet installed a d-doobrie inside each piano so that they would p-play as soon as I named the music. The p-piano only responded to my voice. In return, I ran errands – p-popped to the post office, p-planted explosives, that s-sort of thing.'

I think back to Christmas Eve – to the man in black with the holey gloves, the lost umbrella covered in traces of gunpowder and rosin.

'It was you at the Royal Opera House, wasn't it? You set off the fireworks! But why?'

She gets up off her knees. 'Mr Kinsmeet has taken c-care of me for sixteen years – I'd do anything for him! He's too c-clever for you, Milly K-kydd. He's too c-clever for everyone.'

My eyes dart to the light leaking through the curtains. The golden glow of a new day. Where's Winifred?

Miss Batty follows my gaze. 'There's no p-point in thinking someone's g-going to rescue you. You'll never d-defeat the Mouse King! Not once he has the Nutcracker!'

'You know where it is?'

'Yes, and it will soon be b-back with its master!'

I grab her sleeve. 'Where is it? Where is the Nutcracker?'

With one great tug, she pulls away, leaving her cardigan in my hand. My mouth drops open. Underneath the thick, brown wool, Miss Batty is wearing a glittering ivory tutu.

'Well done, Milly,' says a voice from above. 'You've uncovered my Sugar Plum Fairy. Now, please drop the sword, or you'll never see Merv again.'

27

The Dance of the Sugar Plum Fairy

I throw down the sword.

The voice sounds like it's on its tiptoes.

'Mr Kinsmeet?' My eyes look up, down. *Where is he?*

'Ah, Milly. You really are your mother's daughter. In fact, you've succeeded where she failed. Eva never did work out my true identity.'

'But, *why*, Mr Kinsmeet?'

'My dear, from small deeds great trees grow, and so it was with me. Even as a very small boy, I loathed authority. You see, I was so much cleverer and wittier than the adults around me. My parents were Victorians – humourless, blinkered, stifling. I detested them and swore never to have a family of my own. Once I'd disposed of them, I was free to spread my branches. With my inheritance, I was able to study, to learn, to spend time and money on my inventions. I resolved to dedicate my life to my work

– my *doobries* would be my legacy.'

Miss Batty claps. 'W-well said, Mr Kinsmeet. W-well said!'

'Of course the stars aligned when I was employed by Swan House. It was so easy to create discord in the world, then provide Swan House with the weapons to fight it. The Mouse King created conflict and Hugo Kinsmeet reaped the rewards. Oh, Milly, the gratitude! The respect! The honours! What fun I've had over the years.'

He lets out a long sigh. 'Alas, one has very little fun as one gets older and as my retirement loomed, I became afraid. What fun would there be in leaving all this behind? So I created a weapon in my own image – it had my intelligence, my knowledge, my personality. You can't imagine the pleasure it gave me knowing that on the night of my retirement, I would unveil it to Swan House as a parting gift, knowing that it was as disdainful of authority as I. Knowing that it would create its own mischief. In my absence, my favourite child, my *Nutcracker*, would become Lord of Swan House and King of the World . . .' His voice trails away. 'But there was a problem. Someone had seen through my plan . . .'

Miss Batty tuts beside me. 'S-stupid man. He should n-never have interfered.'

'Actually, Janet, he was the opposite of stupid.

Dear, dear Trevor. He never gave up – try, try and try again.'

My mouth drops open. 'Trevor? Trevor Topping stopped you? But how?'

The voice sighs. 'As you know, Trevor's was my first attempt at an avatar. We remained in touch when he left school and began to work in the field. Unbeknownst to me, he was investigating the Mouse King. He unearthed the article about my parents' demise in the prank that went delightfully right.'

'It was *your* parents that died in the house fire?' My voice is squished with horror. 'Y-you're Mungoe Thiske.'

'Yes, my dear. Mungoe Thiske – Hugo Kinsmeet – The Mouse King – all anagrams, of course. I know you've read the article. It was the one piece of evidence I missed when I reinvented myself and erased Mungoe from history. But I'm not going to be too hard on myself, Milly. I have no regrets.'

Mr Kinsmeet's voice tiptoes up my spine. 'You see, on the night of my retirement party, Trevor discovered the Nutcracker. Not only that, he realized its potential. He hid the laptop on which I had built the malware in a vault protected by a unique defence. Only three people held the key. The two others, Nora Doone and Lord Astus, were both dead.'

'So you killed him,' I whisper. 'You killed Trevor.'

'A messy business – believe me when I say it gave me no pleasure. He was going to reveal my identity and my plan. Fortunately, one of the tunnels under Swan House leads to the zoo. Miss Batty was kind enough to dispose of the body. But thanks to dear Trevor, the Nutcracker was out of my reach for ever . . . or so I thought.'

An image of Miss Batty pushing poor dead Trevor through the tunnels in one of Cook's cake trolleys pops into my head. I shake it out and squint through the window. Where is the Captain? Why are they taking so long? I have to keep Mr Kinsmeet talking.

'S-so what made you come back now?'

'Well, that's where you come in, my dear girl.'

'Me?'

'You and young Tom Garrick.'

'I don't understand . . .'

'Let me enlighten you. Before he left school last term, Tom unearthed one of my favourite doobries – the DC20 I made especially for your mother. I always feared her, you see. I thought if anyone would uncover the truth, she would. So I invented a unique pair of compact drones.'

'A pair? But Mum only had one.'

'Eva had one, and I had the other. The drone, as you know, is a camera. What you don't know is that everything your mother's DC20 films is relayed to me. Everything it sees, I can view via its pair.'

My stomach churns. All the times I used the compact, Mr Kinsmeet was watching.

'When Tom filmed the floor pattern in Astus's *The Secrets of Swan House*, I realized the floor pattern was the key to the vault. *NSKA BLCN BSRE – Dance of Death* – it's a simple enough code to crack. You can imagine my excitement! My wait was over. The Mouse King was AWOKEN.'

A flash of gold darts around the chandelier – a compact drone just like Mum's. *That's* where his voice is coming from – he's communicating through his drone.

'I have enjoyed watching you treasure it, Milly! I have played a game with you and I have won. Draw back the rug, Janet.'

The middle of the wooden floor is covered by a huge, round rug. As Miss Batty rolls it back, I see a steel circle set into the floor. The Swan House motto is engraved around the perimeter, and at its centre is a door.

Underneath the steel floor is the Nutcracker, Hugo Kinsmeet's evil child.

'Lord Astus's vault, Milly. It can only be opened by dancing a precise series of steps. I think you know which dance I mean.'

'Sugar Plum's *manège*,' I whisper.

'Clever girl. I had asked Janet to oblige me, but there was a distinct possibility that she would fail. It was very convenient of Mr Deverall to teach you the dance this term. I'm delighted that you will now be my Sugar Plum.'

'Me?' I fall back, but Miss Batty grabs my arm.

'No. I won't do it!'

The drone drops down to eye level. 'If you refuse to dance, Merv will suffer a similar fate to that of dear Trevor. The lion enclosure would be a fitting resting place, don't you agree?'

I shake off Miss Batty's grip. *Think, Milly, think!*

'Let Merv go first, and then I'll dance for you.' That was a definite nine out of ten on the fib-o-meter.

'My dear Milly. There's a saying – you can't kid a kidder – even with a name like yours. You will dance the *manège* or Merv will die.'

'But I don't have *pointe* shoes. I can't dance Sugar Plum without going *en pointe*!'

'Miss Batty, would you be so kind as to pass Milly a pair of shoes from the selection on the desk to your right. They are from the Astus family's private collection.'

Under a dusty glass cloche on the desk are three pairs of pink satin *pointe* shoes.

Miss Batty chooses a pair. 'Size four, if I remember right. P-put them on.'

'You promise to let Merv go if I dance?'

'Have I ever lied to you, Milly?' says Mr Kinsmeet. 'I give you my word.'

My hands shake as I tie the ribbons. What should I do? I'm in a lose-lose situation. If I refuse, Hugo Kinsmeet will kill us both, and if I agree, he'll have his Nutcracker. I need to buy us some time.

Where, oh where is the Captain?

'Just one more thing, my dear. You should know that the key to the vault was named the Dance of Death for a reason. One mistake will trigger the defence mechanism.'

'What do you mean?'

'One mistake, and you will fry.'

My mouth goes dry. My legs seize up. I've never danced the Sugar Plum without making a mistake, ever. How am I going to do it when my legs are as wobbly as Cook's blancmange? Then Trevor's cheery voice whispers in my ear. *'Don't give up, Milly. Try, try, try again.'*

'Time to take your position, my dear. Please stand on the "C" for Cygni. Miss Batty, perhaps you would accompany Milly on the pianoforte?'

'Of c-course, Mr Kinsmeet.'

Miss Batty sits at the grand piano. She lifts the lid and her fingers hover over the keys.

'"Dance of the Sugar Plum Fairy",' she says.

I close my eyes and force myself to think back to classes with Max. All those instructions he gave Leonora – her flawless dancing.

If she can do it, so can I. I have to.

Miss Batty starts to play. I imagine the celeste tinkling like raindrops on glass. I imagine my Swan-suit is glittering tulle, my hair crowned with tiny white pearls. I imagine I'm Leonora spinning round and around, my arms soft as candy floss, my feet light as clouds. I imagine I *am* the Queen of Christmas.

Max told Leonora to deepen her *plié* before the final step.

Lungs bursting, toes squashed in their unfamiliar shoes, I deepen my *plié* and grit my teeth. What did he say? *Blow the finish and it's game over.*

When the music dies, I fold like a soggy cardigan. The floor beneath me begins to tremble.

'Bravo, Milly!' says Mr Kinsmeet. 'It's opening!'

Not daring to move, I watch the doors grind apart. A deep, dark gap widens beneath me.

'Quickly, my laptop is in a green leather case. If you want to see Merv again, fetch me my Nutcracker!'

Leaping to one side, I tentatively peer over the edge. The vault is deep, big enough to conceal a grand piano. Still panting hard, I lower myself inside.

A musty old smell fills my nose.

265

My hands fumble around each dark and dusty corner. 'I can't see it.'

Hugo's drone whirrs over my shoulder, light shining in my eyes.

'It must be here. What have you done with it?'

'Nothing!' I sit back on my heels. 'It's not here. The vault is empty.'

28

A Matter of Life and Death

'NO!' cries Hugo. 'It's a trick. You're hiding it. Search her, Janet, search her!'

Miss Batty scrambles down beside me.

'I've done my part,' I say. 'So where is he? WHERE'S MERV?'

'We haven't g-got him,' says Miss Batty. 'We j-just said that so you'd help us.'

Suddenly, the vault begins to rumble, the doors begin to close. Miss Batty seizes my wrist but I twist out of her grasp. In the scuffle, my Swanphone falls to the floor, but there's no time to grab it – the gap is narrowing.

Mr Kinsmeet chokes. 'Tell me she's lying!'

Miss Batty drops to her hands and knees and scrabbles around in the corners. 'It must be here . . . it must be . . . I d-don't understand.'

'Find it, Janet. Find my beautiful Nutcracker . . .' A deathly rattle of breath and bones comes from the drone.

'Mr Kinsmeet!' cries Miss Batty.

The light from the drone dims and it crashes to the steel floor, smashing into a hundred golden pieces. I clamber out, but I can't leave Miss Batty trapped in the vault.

'Quickly, Miss Batty. I'll help you out.'

'I can't,' she wails, scooping up wires and springs. 'I've g-got to find the Nutcracker.'

'But it's not here, please Miss Batty.'

I snatch back my outstretched hand just in time. The vault snaps shut. 'Miss Batty!'

There's no response, but behind a curtain there's a snort, a snore, a rasp.

Mr Kinsmeet!

I grab the sword and draw back the curtain with the tip of my blade.

A grubby trainer flumps out. Then another. The trainers are attached to a pair of old jeans. I tug the curtain back. The jeans are attached to . . .

'MERV!'

Merv's eyes are shut and his mouth is open.

'Merv, wake up!

Merv stirs. 'Beam me up, Shcotty.'

'Scotty? Merv, are you all right?'

'Leave me alone – I'm taking a lickle nap.'

I pat his cheek. It's slightly sticky with dribble.

'Merv, please, the Nutcracker – it's gone!'

Merv sits up. 'The Nutcracker?'

'Yes. It was in the vault and now it's gone.'

'There's shomething I need to tell you 'bout that . . .' Merv puffs out his cheeks. 'But my tongue feelsh funny.'

'Do you know where it is?'

'What?'

'The NUTCRACKER!'

'I found it.'

Thank Crump for that! 'Where is it?'

'Where'sh what?'

'Come on, Merv, this is a matter of life and death. Where did you find the Nutcracker?'

Merv smiles a lopsided smile. 'I forgot.'

I try another tack. 'What happened to you?'

Merv moans. 'I wuz *zzz*ipped. IT WUZ HORRIBLE!'

'By who? Merv, who zipped you?'

'I shaw them shneak through the theatre sho I followed them an' there she wuz – twirling an' twirling an' there wuz a big hole in the floor an' they took out a case an' then . . .' Merv shudders. 'They *zzzzzzzzz* . . .'

'No!' I grab both his shoulders. 'Merv – don't go back to sleep. WHO ZIPPED YOU? WHO ARE YOU TALKING ABOUT?'

Merv blinks. 'Aren't you lishning? It wuz the *Deverallsh*. Max and Leonora. They *zzz*ipped me an' now they're gunna get away . . .'

I'm so confused. If my head was spinning before, it's about to fall off now.

'But Max isn't the Mouse King. Are you sure it was the Deveralls?'

'Who?' says Merv.

Garghhh!

Is that why Max spent all his time rehearsing the Sugar Plum Fairy? Is that why he gave Leonora all of his attention – so she could open the vault?

'Shcotty?' says Merv. 'Can you beam me back to the Enterprishe now . . .'

I roll my eyes. 'Aye, aye, Captain.'

As Merv goes back to snoring, I peer out of the window. Down in the frost-white courtyard, a rumble is building from Ms Celia's coach house.

A red sports car noses out of the garage. It revs its engine then zooms towards the main entrance. The roof is down and I glimpse the driver's face.

Sugar Plum Fairies! It's Max Deverall. And he's getting away!

My feet are so stumbly I can barely stand up, but I stagger back through the theatre, down the staircase and tumble into the lobby. I reach the car park just as the car screeches on to the drive.

Then everything happens at once.

Earnest bunny-hops from the lawn and creaks across the gravel. Spencer flings open his door into the path of the speeding car. The red convertible rises up on two wheels, bounces down, and swerves to a stop.

'Well done, Spencer!' I yell, running on to the drive.

Spencer gives me a thumbs up from the driving seat.

Inside the car are three shocked faces. One with burning bonfire eyes. One with her mother's lips and one I've never seen before.

I'm still staring into the dazed and impossibly beautiful face of Juliet Sarova when a roar overhead startles us both.

Winifred!

I search the early-morning sky, but the looming white dot is too small to be Winifred. It lands on the drive, light as a butterfly, and seconds later, a woman jumps on to the gravel.

'Mum!'

'Milly, you're back, thank God.' She wraps me in her arms. 'I'm so sorry. When I heard Max had escaped I came as soon as I could. The Captain's not here yet?'

'No. We had to leave Casova before them.'

'Don't worry, they've been sighted over the Channel, they'll be back soon.' Her eyes narrow at Max's passenger. 'Is that Juliet Sarova, Max? You've got a lot of explaining to do.'

Max smiles his superstar smile. 'I will if you just give me a chance.'

I pull away. 'Don't listen to him, Mum. They came back for the Nutcracker. It was in the school all along.'

Max's smile falters. 'Did you just say the Nutcracker's *here*?'

'You should know. You took the laptop from the vault.'

'Just one second. Milly, I'm NOT the Mouse King!'

'I know that, Hugo Kinsmeet is – *was* – I'm not sure, he might be a bit dead. The Nutcracker malware's on his laptop.'

'Hugo?' say Mum and Max together.

'I'll explain in a minute – the thing is, Merv saw you. You *zipped* him!'

Max holds up his hands. 'I admit I zipped your friend – on the absolutely lowest setting of a pre-Swanphone model, I promise – but the *Nutcracker*? No way.'

'I've heard enough, Max,' says Mum. 'Open the boot.'

Max sighs. 'Look, we took a case from the vault, OK? But I swear Merv arrived before we had a chance to look inside.'

'Stay back, Milly,' says Mum as she slowly, steadily, carefully opens the boot. She finds the green leather case.

'Milly's right. It's Hugo's laptop. How long have you known it was in the school?'

Max's cheeks are villain white. 'I didn't know it was in there!'

I say to Mum, 'If he didn't know about the Nutcracker, why would he take something from the vault?'

'Max?' says Mum.

Max shakes his head. 'It was a sham, Eva. Leo and I are tired. We're tired of the travel, the lying, the danger. We're tired of the traitors, the trouble, those lethal flying tutus. We've had too many near misses. I want to do a little fishing, grow my own veg, play a little golf . . .'

Leonora sobs. 'And I want to stop moving. I want to go to school and make *friends*.'

'Oh, Leonora.' Mum's eyes are shiny, like sequins.

Max glances back at Juliet. 'When I met Juliet, I realized that unless I found some way for us to disappear, we'd never have a chance at a regular life. Creating new identities is an expensive business.

Then I remembered what Nora'd said about the vault before she'd died. She'd set the defence for the last Lord Astus when she was still at school. I thought it would be full of the family silver, so we decided to take what we needed and run. '

Leonora says, 'It was all going to plan, but then the Mouse King sent you the doll and there was no way we could abandon you with the mission coming up, so we decided to leave in half-term instead.'

Max glances back at me. 'I knew things would be tricky with Milly around, especially if she and Leo got close, so I ordered Leo not to let that happen.'

'Sorry, Milly, I wanted to be friends, but . . .' Leonora hangs her head.

'I'm sorry too, Eva,' says Max. 'I promised you I wouldn't let Milly go to Casova, but there was nothing I could do. She's one determined kid.'

'Is that true, Mum?'

'I was too far away to protect you, Milly. Max promised to keep you safe.'

'That's the only promise I've broken,' says Max. 'I swear I didn't know the Nutcracker was in the case.'

'Mum,' I say, watching Leonora's spy-face unravel. 'They're telling the truth.'

'That might be the case, but even if they didn't intend to steal the Nutcracker, this is still theft. I'm sorry, Max. It means prison, and Leonora will have to be taken away.'

'Mum, no—'

A hum fills the sky. Mum shields her eyes. Glinting against the pale blue is another convertible. Relief washes over me.

Lottie.

'Did you say something, sweetheart?'

I point at the case in Mum's hand. 'You've got the Nutcracker, so Max hasn't actually taken anything, has he? And Ms Celia's got so many convertibles she's not going to miss this one.'

'What are you saying, Milly?'

'Can't we let them go? Max and Juliet, I mean, not Leonora.' I meet Leonora's eyes. 'Now she's settled in and everything, I think Leonora should stay here in Swan House. She's brilliant, Mum – a superspy. We need her.'

'Can I, Dad?' says Leonora.

'But, Leo – all the plans we made . . .'

'*You* made, Dad. I like it here! Please, I need friends of my own age.'

Mum glances up at Winifred, then does the tiniest nod. 'Hurry, Max, you'd better go before I change my mind.'

Leonora leans over to hug her dad and Juliet before clambering out of the car. Mum and I get a hug too. It smells of sugar plum fairies.

Then the engine revs, the roof purrs over Max's head, and fins slide out of sides.

'I won't forget this, Milly, I always knew you were a star!' shouts Max. 'I'll be in touch, Leo. Look after each other!'

Max's jaw wobbles and he gives one last wave. The car squeals right and zooms towards the lake. I take Leonora's hand as it launches into the water, bubbling for a moment before it sinks out of sight.

There's a shout from the lawn. 'I love a happy ending but what about me?'

Leonora laughs. 'I s'pose we'd better free Spencer.'

'I s'pose we better had.'

As we wriggle Spencer free, Lottie and the Captain come thundering across the lawn. Jada and Bumble are close behind.

'Does someone want to tell me what's going on? Did I just see Deverall steal a convertible?'

'It's all right, Captain,' says Mum. 'There'd been a misunderstanding. Max is taking a long vacation. And look –' she holds up the case – 'Milly found the Nutcracker. It was here all along.'

'The credit should go to Trevor,' I say, smiling at Lottie.

Lottie grins her dimply grin. 'Not Try-try-try-again Toppin'!'

'It's a long story, but first we'd better check on

Merv.' I hook one arm in Lottie's and the other in Leonora's. 'And we'll need you to open the vault again, Leo – my legs are like jelly.'

'Why's that?' asks Leonora.

'Miss Batty's trapped inside.'

'You've got to be jokin'!' says Lottie.

'Like I said, it's a long story.'

29

The Nutcracker

Mum asks Jada to help Spencer to the infirmary. The rest of us troop into the school. The Captain leads the way, carrying the green leather briefcase like it's a sleeping baby.

As we walk through the lobby, I tell everyone about Hugo Kinsmeet and how Trevor Topping fooled him. 'You told me Trevor was clever,' I say to Leonora. 'Sorry, I should have listened.'

'Don't apologize. If it wasn't for you, Dad and I would be on our way to prison.' Leonora blushes like a normal person. 'I know what we did was wrong, but we needed the money to start again. Dad promised me he was going to pay it all back as soon as he'd found a job.'

'Yeah, right,' says Bumble.

'Shut up, Bumble,' says Lottie.

'But I still don't get why he didn't just tell the Captain about Juliet.'

'I wish he had,' says Leonora. 'But he didn't want me to know about her until he was sure she'd come with us. It's been just the two of us for so long, I think he was scared of telling me. He thought I'd be hurt or jealous or something . . .' She glances at me. 'But I'm glad he met Juliet. I wanted him to find someone so he wouldn't need me so much – I wanted to make friends of my own.' She checks Mum is out of earshot. 'To be honest, Milly, at first I thought it was your mum he'd fallen for.'

'Me too,' I say. 'That's why I got so mad at you. Mum's away so much I didn't want to share her. I was the one who was hurt and jealous. Sorry I was so horrible.'

'I think I was pretty annoying too.' Leonora gives me an apologetic smile.

Bumble nods. 'Sooo annoying.'

We reach the bottom of the staircase. 'Wait a moment,' says Mum. 'Captain, have you any idea why our Swanphones aren't working.'

The Captain shakes his ponytail beard. 'It's not just our Swanphones. Everything's down.'

'Strange,' says Mum. 'Girls, you go to the vault and fetch Miss Batty and Merv. I'll go to the CR and reboot the mainframe. Captain, come with me – I'd really like to try out the new sensor once our phones are working.'

Up in Lord Astus's apartment, Merv is still fast asleep. Bumble gives him a poke.

'Poor Merv,' says Leonora. 'Dad really didn't mean to hurt him.'

'He'll live,' says Bumble. She empties her utility belt and grins at the doobries. 'One of these should wake him up.'

Leonora pulls out a pair of *pointe* shoes from her backpack and takes her place on the steel floor.

'Are you sure you can do it?' I say, remembering what Hugo said about the Dance of Death.

'I'm sure – I've been practising Sugar Plum for ever.'

I count her in with a nervous, *one, two, three, four*, but I needn't have worried. Lottie and I watch in awe as Leonora dances with deft, death-defying precision. I sigh. She's so brave.

Lottie claps as a crack appears at Leonora's feet. Stepping back from the widening gap, she holds up her wrist. 'Look, Milly, our Swanphones are working. Your mum must have turned the mainframe back on.'

Merv groans. 'Did someone say mainframe?'

'That's weird,' says Lottie, approaching the vault.

'I just turned on the sensor, and . . .' She frowns at the angry green light flashing on her wrist.

Merv bolts upright. 'NOOOO!'

The vault doors grate back and a ghostly green glow escapes the darkness. Lottie peers inside.

'Get back!' shouts Merv.

Too late. A thin green ray shoots from the vault. Leonora and I duck but the light hits Lottie in the chest. It lifts her off her feet and throws her into Bumble.

Leonora leaps behind the piano. I dive to the floor.

My heart thunders in my chest. 'Lottie! Are you OK?'

'Flamin' Nora,' mumbles Lottie, flopping next to Merv.

'She's been zipped,' says Bumble, pinning a squirming Merv to the ground. 'It's OK, she's laughing.'

I creep towards the vault. 'Miss Batty, no one will hurt you if you just come out with your hands up.'

A giggle echoes around the vault. My skin crawls.

It doesn't sound like Miss Batty.

It doesn't sound entirely human.

'Kydd, stay down!' says Merv.

I crawl to the edge of the vault and peep down. Miss Batty and her sparkly tutu are slumped against the wall. My eyes stretch wide. Shimmering in the opposite corner is my mentor.

'Trevor? What are you doing there?'

'Greetings, Milly,' he beams. 'What can I do for you?'

'Just tell me what happened. Is Miss Batty – is she dead?'

'Ahh, sorry about that. I don't know what came over me. To be perfectly honest, I'm not quite sure how I got here.'

'Milly, get back,' warns Leonora.

'It's OK. Trevor's my mentor, he won't hurt me.' I point at the green flashing light next to Miss Batty's hand. 'Trevor, my Swanphone's down there. Maybe it activated you by accident?'

There's a whimper from under Bumble's armpit. 'It's not an accident. We're all DOOMED!'

'What are you on about, Merv?' says Bumble.

'I remember – I remember why I switched off the mainframe!'

'You switched it off – why?'

'The Nutcracker's inside Trevor's avatar,' says Merv.

'Is it?' says Trevor, before popping into thin air.

'What did you say?'

'Has he gone?' says Merv, wiping the sweat from his monobrow. 'I figured it all out when I was trying to fix Trevor's avatar. There's a worm in his software – powerful malware that's been there since Kinsmeet retired. When Kydd was paired with Trevor, the genie was let out of the bottle. Then I realized that Hugo Kinsmeet is an anagram of the Mouse King. Put two and two together and you get the Nutcracker.'

I think about Trevor's cat-green eyes just like Hugo Kinsmeet's. It was a clue and I missed it.

'So that's why Trevor wasn't functioning properly.'

'Yes, and that's why I turned off the mainframe,' says Merv. 'I had to stop the Nutcracker taking over Trevor completely. Eventually it would have infected the whole of the MNTR programme.'

Near the piano, Leonora shudders. 'And I guess it wouldn't have stopped there – it could have taken over the entire network.'

'There'sh got to be shumfink we can do to shtop it,' groans Lottie.

'The only way is to turn off the mainframe again,' says Merv. 'At least that'll give us enough time to figure out what to do next.'

'I'll go!' I say.

'YOU'RE NOT GOING ANYWHERE!' I jump as Trevor reappears at the edge of the vault. His eyes flash like traffic lights. His mouth is filled with neon green light. His body glows with a menacing green aura.

'T-Trevor?'

'Do not insult me. I am THE NUTCRACKER!'

'B-but how did you get inside Trevor?'

'Dear Trevor Topping put me here himself.'

'I-I don't understand. Mr Kinsmeet said you were on his laptop and that's why Trevor'd hidden it in the vault.'

'That is partly true. When he failed to destroy me, he resorted to moving my malware into a long-forgotten folder containing the early protype of his avatar. As an extra precaution, he sealed my maker's laptop in the vault.'

I look into Bad Trevor's eyes. '*Trevor?*' I plead. 'Trevor, come back. You're still in there somewhere.'

Bad Trevor's face screws up. 'SILENCE! I AM THE NUTCR—'

The avatar fizzes and pops. It splutters and splinters. It blinks on and off like a twinkling green star.

'Milly, gosh. Sorry about that,' says Good Trevor. 'I'm afraid it's not looking good. The malware inside me is too powerful . . .'

'Trevor, please – try, try, try again, remember?'

Trevor scratches his head. 'Wait a minute – there might be a way . . .'

'Tell me,' I say as he starts breaking up.

'The weapon . . . was modelled on its . . . maker. If you think about Mr Kinsmeet's . . . strengths and . . . weaknessessssSSS*SILENCE!*'

Bad Trevor's back, pointing his glowing green fingers and sizzling with pulsating power. 'Hugo gave me his wit, his cunning, his intellect, and then multiplied it by a thousand! I HAVE NO WEAKNESSES!'

I have to say, I totally believe him.

But what did Good Trevor mean? I rack my brains – I hardly knew Mr Kinsmeet. What were his weaknesses?

Then, in the corner of my eye, I notice Leonora crawl under the piano. She's making her way to the door. *Think, Milly!* I have to distract Bad Trevor so Leonora can slip out.

There's a waspish whisper from under the window. 'A riddle, Milly,' says Bumble. 'Use a riddle.'

A riddle? OF COURSE! The Mouse King was a joker – he couldn't resist a riddle. Maybe, just maybe, someone's strength can also be their weakness?

30

Heroes and Heroines

'OK, prove it!' I say to Bad Trevor. 'Prove how clever you are. I challenge you to solve the most difficult riddle in the world.'

Bad Trevor's eyes narrow. 'The most difficult riddle in the world? Ha! I accept your challenge!'

I squeeze my eyes shut, wishing with every fibre of my being that I'd paid more attention in class. 'It's . . . it's . . . it's . . .'

'Patience is not one of my virtues,' says Bad Trevor.

Bumble and Leonora would be so much better at this than me. Leonora's so clever and brave and— Wait a minute . . . 'I've got it!'

'This better be good,' mutters Bumble.

'I'm waiting,' says Bad Trevor.

'Er, it's a word.'

'Like I said, doomed,' says Merv.

I square my shoulders and look Bad Trevor in his

impossibly evil eyes. 'It's the word that's going to DESTROY you.'

'DESTROY ME?'

Sparks flash across the room. The stink of singed hair goes up my nose. 'Ignorant, snivelling human. TELL ME THE RIDDLE!'

'Tell him the blooming riddle!' squeaks Merv, batting smoke from his monobrow.

I take a deep breath, not daring to check on Leonora. I don't suppose our Swansuits are Nutcracker proof. If Bad Trevor spots her trying to escape, she won't be toast – she'll be the little burnt breadcrumbs at the bottom of the toaster.

'OK. The first two letters relate to a boy. The first three letters relate to a girl. The first four letters relate to Trevor. And ALL the letters relate to Leonora.'

Bad Trevor's shoulders begin to shake. Is he *laughing*?

'What's so funny?'

'That's EASY-PEASY!' says Bad Trevor, sounding way too pleased with himself. 'It's the EASIEST PEASIEST riddle in the world! I shall answer your riddle, and then you will DIE!'

I slide my eyes over to Bumble. *Where's Leonora?* they say. But Bumble's eyes are glued to Bad Trevor.

'THIS IS THE ANSWER!' crows Bad Trevor. 'The

first two letters make *HE*. The first three letters make *HER* . . . you were trying to trick me with the rest, but I have seen through your feeble wordplay. The first four letters spell *HERO*. And the whole word spells . . .'

He points a deadly green finger. 'HEROINE!'

Drat.

'Prepare to be wiped from the universe!'

'NOOO!' I dive in front of my friends.

A heartbeat of silence is filled with a blinding green flash. Sparks shoot from the ceiling. Droplets of glass rain down . . . then everything goes quiet.

I feel my nose, my chin, my cheeks. I'm still here. So is Bumble. Merv and I both open our eyes. There's no sign of Bad Trevor. Or Good Trevor. Or Leonora.

'Get off me, will you? He's gone.' Bumble shakes bits of chandelier out of her hair.

'Wish I could move my legsh,' says Lottie as I whoop and twirl and fist-bump Bumble.

'Leonora did it!' I say. 'She turned off the main-frame.'

'You did say she was a heroine,' grunts Merv.

Bumble smiles the right way round. 'Yeah, but *sooo* annoying.'

The wheels of the cab crunch over the gravel as we drive past the gate house. The cabbie catches my eye in the mirror. 'I know you, don't I? Drove you to Swan 'ouse last September. You was a ballerina if I remember right.'

'That's right,' I say, happily squished between Mum and Bab.

'Told my youngest about this place,' he says. 'Said if he worked at his ballet, he might end up here one day.' He grins as Swan House comes into view. A perfect white mansion on a perfect green lawn.

It's been fourteen days since we found the Nutcracker. Afterwards, we were sent home until Ms Celia had sorted out things in Westminster. That meant two whole weeks of just Mum, Bab and me.

Plus Leonora, of course.

And Merv. His mum was still on her honeymoon so he stayed in our attic. To be honest, we didn't see him much. Turned out Merv was more scared of Boris than he was of the Nutcracker.

Bab said I could bring Boris to show Lottie. He's purring on Merv's lap, clinging to his jumper like a fat ginger limpet.

'Help me,' squeaks Merv.

Leonora laughs and pulls Boris off.

Merv stares at the holes in his jumper. 'I've been punctured.'

Mum hides a smile. 'That means he likes you.'

As the cabbie pulls over, Merv mutters something about tetanus jabs and hurls himself out, straight into Lottie and Spencer.

Mum slides out with Leonora and I call out to Lottie. 'Lottie! Come and meet Boris and my babushka.'

Lottie clambers inside and gives them both a hug.

'I've heard so much about you, dahhling,' says Bab. 'You must come to stay in the summer holidays. Ve've had such fun with Leonora, haven't ve, Mila? And vhat vas the name of the boy vith the thermos?'

'Merv,' I say.

'Yes, and Merv too. You vill come, von't you?' says Bab.

'You bet!' grins Lottie.

'Wish you'd been with us,' I say. 'We got back in time for the last day of Winter Wonderland. Leo and I did the Ho-Ho-Helterskelter three times.'

Leonora also showed me how to perfect my unreadable spy-face and I showed her how to staple an origami gag.

'It was the best holiday ever,' I say, meaning every word.

The sun blinks from behind the clouds as we wave off Bab and Boris.

Inside the lobby there's laughter as William Flynn

shows some of the boys his straightened nose. The laughter stops when Mum walks past.

'Look over there – it's Eva Kydd!' says a small boy with a greasy fringe and an impish grin. He winks as I pass by.

Tom Garrick's broken ankle must be better. Honestly, he has no idea what he started.

'Milly, wait!' says a waspish voice behind us.

I turn and catch Bumble's hand. 'Come on! We'll be late.'

'Just a moment,' says the lady behind her.

Bumble's mum gives her a hug. 'Bye then, love. See you at half-term.'

'Where are the triplets?' I ask when she's gone.

'Started nursery,' says Bumble with a sigh. 'I almost miss them.'

The theatre is packed. Mum leaves me with my friends and makes her way to the stage. Awed whispers follow her down the aisle like the pitter-patter of raindrops.

'Do you fink we've got a new mission?' says Lottie.

Merv groans. 'Hope not. I'm still scarred from the last one.'

'Scarred? Let's see,' says Bumble in her happy voice.

'Gettin' zipped ain't that bad,' grins Lottie.

Onstage, Ms Celia seems springier – like a bit of Max Deverall has brushed off on her. She's even wearing red lipstick.

'Good morning, everyone, and welcome back. Let me begin by putting your minds at rest with regard to the Nutcracker. It is now securely contained in the vault, and a new key has been created. We are confident that poor Miss Batty will be its first and *last* victim.'

I frown at Leonora, who frowns at Lottie, who frowns at Spencer. He raises his hand. 'But, I thought you said you were going to destroy it.'

'I will, in time, of course. But for now, it's been agreed that such a unique weapon should be studied. I can assure you, it is perfectly safe.'

Safe? I cross my fingers and cling on to hope like a fat ginger cat clings on to a *Star Trek* jumper.

'What about the Mouse King, Miss Celia?' asks Jada Gayle.

'Hugo Kinsmeet's whereabouts are currently unknown. A search is ongoing, but we believe he is no longer a threat.' Ms Celia digs inside her trouser pocket. 'And now to the real reason I've gathered you here.' She holds up a blue velvet box. 'This is the Leonis medal – our highest award for valour. To present the award is someone you will all recognize.'

Mum steps on to the stage.

'It will surprise most of you to know that Eva Kydd has been involved with Swan House for some time, and is well aware of our work. It will also surprise you to know that she has agreed to be our new Head of Ballet.'

Everyone stamps and cheers. Lottie and Leonora squeeze my arms. I told them the second Mum said she'd decided to step down as O and take over from Max. Max and Juliet had made her reassess her position, she said. It was about time she gave more time to the people she loved most.

Mum takes the box from Ms Celia. 'It gives me great pleasure to present the Leonis medal to a very deserving member of the Swan House family.'

She beckons into the wings and a lady wanders on to the stage. 'Come on, Emmie,' the lady says. 'Don't leave me by myself.'

Blimey, it's Cook! 'Doesn't she look lovely without her blue hairnet?' whispers Leonora.

Topsy sidles onstage next to her. They straighten down their tops and fiddle with their hair. Topsy is pinker than ever.

Mum opens the box. 'Trevor Topping sacrificed his life to save others. In the end, it was his deep humility and die-hard spirit that enabled him to outsmart the Mouse King. Mrs Topping – Emmeline – I would like you to accept this medal on behalf of one of the bravest men Swan House has ever known.'

A shiny gold medal dangles from Mum's fingers. 'To unsung heroes – *Cycni venustas, cor leonis*!'

She puts the medal around Cook's neck and starts to clap.

We all stand up. I clap for Trevor, I clap for heroes. I clap for heroines, I clap for friends. I clap for Max and Juliet. I hope wherever they are, it's a million miles from traitors and trouble and Madge's lethal, flying tutus.

Acknowledgements

I owe enormous thanks to lots of kind, talented people, and one beautiful, if batty, old dog.

To the lovely folk at Chicken House – Barry Cunningham, Rachel Leyshon, Laura Myers, Jazz Bartlett Love, Elinor Bagenal, Sarah Wallis-Newman, Esther Waller and Fraser Crichton for dusting off Milly's tutu and launching her on a second trouble-packed adventure. To my editor Kesia Lupo for her insight and imagination. To Rachel Hickman and Helen Crawford-White for a cracking Christmassy cover.

To my agent, Nicola Barr for being brilliant at all the things I'm not.

To the Bath Spa MAWP class of 2016 for being top listeners, with special thanks to Sarah, Kathryn and Julie.

To Charlie at Urban Writers' Retreat for peace, quiet and excellent dinners.

To the McBrydes, my beloved Hughsies and all my family in South Wales.

To Evie for all my best ideas.

To Rog, Rory and Drew for making anything possible.

To my awesome readers.

To the Royal Ballet for continuing to inspire,

entertain and educate. I hope you're back wowing live audiences very soon.

And to the NHS and key workers in Gloucestershire, thank you for keeping me safe and well while I finished this book.